"Do you ever wonder...was it really as good as we remember?"

Her words rocked through him.

Her gaze fell to his mouth. "It was just the adrenaline, right? The danger? The whole life-or-death situation that we were in. I mean...there's no way that we'd kiss again and—"

"Ignite?"

Her lips parted.

He wanted her mouth. He also wanted to show her that he could be more than the rough SEAL she'd known before.

"Yes," she whispered. "Ignite."

Hunger, desire pulsed through him. "You should walk away now."

He'd said words like that to her, before. Another time, another place.

She'd been hugging him, her body trembling. Desire had twisted inside him. He'd tried to do the right thing. Tried to warn her away.

You should walk away.

But she hadn't walked away then. She'd stood on her tiptoes and put her mouth against his.

And now...now she was walking toward him, stopping only when their bodies brushed.

"One kiss...just to find out?"

SECRETS

New York Times Bestselling Author

CYNTHIA EDEN

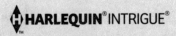

HARLEQUIN® INTRIGUE®

I'd like to offer a huge thanks to Denise and Shannon—it is a pleasure working with you!

For my readers, thank you so much for your support. You've been absolutely incredible! And I hope you enjoy my latest Intrigue.

ISBN-13: 978-0-373-74873-0

Secrets

Copyright © 2015 by Cindy Roussos

Recycling programs for this product may not exist in your area.

Printed in U.S.A.

www.Harlequin.com

Cynthia Eden, a *New York Times* bestselling author, writes tales of romantic suspense and paranormal romance. Her books have received starred reviews from *Publishers Weekly*, and she has received a RITA® Award nomination for best romantic suspense novel. Cynthia lives in the Deep South, loves horror movies and has an addiction to chocolate. More information about Cynthia may be found at cynthiaeden.com, or you can follow her on Twitter, @cynthiaeden.

Books by Cynthia Eden

HARLEQUIN INTRIGUE

The Battling McGuire Boys
Confessions
Secrets

Shadow Agents
Alpha One
Guardian Ranger
Sharpshooter
Glitter and Gunfire

Shadow Agents: Guts and Glory
Undercover Captor
The Girl Next Door
Evidence of Passion
Way of the Shadows

Visit the Author Profile page at Harlequin.com for more titles

CAST OF CHARACTERS

Jennifer Wesley—Jennifer knows that she is in danger. Someone has been stalking her, and if Jennifer can't unmask the man terrorizing her, she fears that she may lose her life. She turns to the only person she can trust...a man who saved her life once before, on a dark and deadly night years ago...

Brodie McGuire—Tough ex-SEAL Brodie McGuire spends his days and nights working to bring down criminals. He's always ready and eager to face danger, but when he learns that Jennifer is being threatened again, he knows that his new case will be very, very personal. He let Jennifer escape from his life once before, and he vows not to make the same mistake again.

Davis McGuire—Brodie's twin, Davis, has followed his brother into more battles than he can count. When Davis sees how quickly Brodie appears to be falling for the mysterious Jennifer, he worries that his brother may be facing a battle that he can't win. Jennifer is a woman with secrets, and Davis is determined to uncover them and protect his brother, at all costs.

Mark Montgomery—Mark has lived next to the McGuires for years, and he was close by the night that the family suffered a terrible tragedy. Yet it seems Mark has been keeping his own secrets, and when Jennifer's attacker targets him, too, those secrets may be dragged out into the harsh light of day.

Shayne Townsend—Detective Shayne Townsend has worked closely with Brodie for years. He knows every detail about the vicious murders that nearly tore apart the McGuire family. As danger threatens the McGuires once more, he wonders if the family will be strong enough to survive.

Prologue

He'd rescued her from hell.

Jennifer Wesley turned slightly, and her gaze fell on the man in bed beside her. Sleep made him look innocent, safe, but she knew that image was a lie.

There was nothing safe about Brodie McGuire. The man was a SEAL. Dangerous. Deadly. A force to be reckoned with.

She'd thought for certain that a rescue wasn't going to happen for her. Her captors had sure been confident that she would never escape from them. Then Brodie had appeared.

Her fingers brushed over his hard jaw, tracing the dark stubble there. His eyes opened at her touch, his green stare 100 percent awake and aware.

He was naked. So was she. After the rescue, once they'd ditched her captors and made it to relative safety, the adrenaline and fear that she'd felt for so long had morphed into something else entirely. The power of her desire had taken Jennifer by surprise.

He hadn't seduced her. Hadn't taken advantage—

she'd been the one so intent on kissing him. On finding some pleasure to push away the nightmares and the terror.

His gaze slowly slid over her face. She had the odd feeling that he was almost…almost trying to memorize her features.

Only fair, really. She didn't want to forget anything about him.

"Thank you," Jennifer whispered.

His dark brows rose.

"For saving me." Not the lovemaking part. She felt her cheeks stain. "I thought I was going to die out there." Her wrists were still red and raw from the rope burns. She tried to smile. "I sure am glad you were the navy SEAL assigned to my case." She was more grateful than words would ever be able to express.

I would have died without him.

"Your father wasn't going to let you vanish," Brodie assured her. She caught the faintest hint of a Texas drawl in his voice. There one moment, gone the next. "He used all his pull to bring in my team."

"My…father?" She kept the emotion from her voice—she'd learned that trick long ago. For her, life was all about acting now. Hiding emotion was necessary for survival.

"Yeah, the oil magnate. He's the reason you were pulled into this mess." Anger roughened his voice for a moment. "Your captors thought they could ransom you for a fortune."

No, they hadn't. They'd just planned to kill her. But there was some information she couldn't tell her rescuer. He didn't have enough clearance to know everything.

Jennifer leaned forward. Her lips brushed across his. "Thank you," she said again.

His arms curled around her as he pulled her up against his body. *Powerful*, *hard*, *hot*—those words perfectly described Brodie. She wanted to just stay there with him. To forget the rest of the world for a while.

But forgetting wasn't an option for her. Especially not when she could hear the pounding of footsteps right outside their safe house.

Gasping, she tried to pull back from him.

"Easy." He let her go and rose to his feet. Brodie jerked on a pair of cargo pants and peered through the thin crack between the window and the long, dark curtain. "It's my men."

His men. Okay, right, but his men could *not* see her naked. Jennifer grabbed for her clothes—bloody and dirty though they were—and she dressed as quickly as she could. When she whirled back around, Brodie was fully dressed, too—looking all crisp and in control, and not at all like a man who'd spent the hours of the night making passionate love to her.

When he opened the door, Jennifer saw that his gun was tucked into the waistband of his pants. Men streamed into the safe house then, men who moved with the same controlled, soundless steps that Brodie used.

"We have a chopper waiting for you, Ms. Wesley," one of those men said. He was tall, with blond hair and bright blue eyes. "You'll be on your way home in less than an hour."

Home. She didn't really have one of those. Her gaze slid back to Brodie. She shouldn't ask this, but Jennifer still heard herself say, "Will you be on the chopper with me?" Because Brodie made her feel safe. In a world of lies, he was a man that she trusted. Someone she could count on.

It wasn't every day that a man risked his life to save her.

But Brodie shook his head. "I have to stay for mission containment. That's your flight to freedom, not mine."

The others were watching them. Did they know what had happened in that safe house? Jennifer felt as if the truth was stamped on her face. *No, it isn't. You never reveal what you feel.*

She closed the distance between them. She rose onto her tiptoes and, putting her mouth close to his ear, asked, "Will I ever see you again?"

His body was so tense against hers. "Hopefully, you won't need to see me."

She eased away from him.

"Try not to get kidnapped again, and you won't need me."

Not get kidnapped? No, she couldn't make that promise. He didn't understand the world she lived in.

Her gaze swept over him. Lingered. He hadn't been what she'd expected, and she wouldn't be forgetting him anytime soon.

Jennifer headed toward the door.

"I'm…I'm sure your father will be glad to see you," Brodie's gruff voice followed her. "He moved heaven and hell to find you."

Glancing back, Jennifer gave him a faint smile. "I'm sure he'll be thrilled when he sees me."

And that would be a miracle, actually, considering that her father had been dead for ten years.

She followed her new guards and slipped out the door. The men with her were saying that she had to hurry, that her safety depended on a quick departure.

So Jennifer didn't glance back. She didn't waste time on goodbyes with Brodie.

Yes, he'd been unexpected…and Jennifer was quite sure that she'd never forget him.

Too bad he had no clue who she really was.

Chapter One

Six years later...

A ghost from his past had just walked right through his office door. Brodie McGuire shook his head, an instinctive response, because he could *not* be seeing that woman. There was no way she was standing there. No way.

Usually she only appeared in his dreams.

She couldn't have just walked into his office at McGuire Securities. She was far away, some place safe and no doubt with—

"We have a walk-in appointment that I was hoping you could handle," Brodie's older brother, Grant, told him. "This is Jennifer—"

"Wesley," Brodie finished, then cleared his throat because that one word had sounded like a growl.

Grant's brows climbed. "You two know each other?"

Yes, they did. Intimately.

"Well, that just makes things easier." Grant

flashed a broad smile. "Ms. Wesley, I will leave you in my brother's capable hands."

Brodie realized that he'd leaped to his feet as soon as he'd gotten a look at Jennifer.

Grant glanced over at him, a faint frown on his face. Brodie offered what he hoped was a reassuring smile as he hurried around his desk and toward Jennifer.

Grant hesitated a moment more; then he slipped from the office. The door shut quietly behind him, and, just like that, Brodie was alone with the woman who'd been in his dreams for far too long.

Brodie almost reached out and touched Jennifer, just to make sure she was really there, but then he remembered the way desire had burned so hot and wild between them before.

To play it safe, he tucked his hands in his pockets and just inclined his head toward her. "Been a long time, Ms. Wesley." He was impressed that his voice came out sounding so calm.

Her laughter sounded the way he'd thought it would. Sweet, light, musical. She hadn't laughed when they'd been together in the Middle East. She'd been far too afraid for laughter. He'd hated her fear, and he was damn glad to see her like this...happy.

"And here I was worried you wouldn't remember me," she murmured. Her smile flashed, a wide, slow smile that made her deep brown eyes light up.

"But I really think you can drop the 'Ms. Wesley' part, don't you?"

Then she made a terrible mistake. She came forward and wrapped her arms around him. Her scent, a light lavender, drifted in the air as she hugged him. He probably shouldn't have wrapped his arms around her and hugged her so tightly. Probably shouldn't have inhaled her scent so greedily. But he did.

She fit against him, perfectly so. He'd thought that before, on that long-ago night.

Jennifer eased back and stared up at him. "You haven't changed. You look exactly the same, even after all this time."

He'd changed plenty. Most of those changes were on the inside, though, because he was good at keeping his mask in place. Brodie forced himself to let her go, when he wanted to hold on to her tightly.

That part hasn't changed, either.

After the night they'd shared together, he'd wanted to grab hold of her and never let go. But the mission had waited. Her *life* had waited.

He eased out a slow breath, and his gaze swept slowly over her face. Her eyes were big, dark, almond-shaped and framed by the longest lashes he'd ever seen. Her hair was a black curtain around her, and her skin was a warm, sun-kissed gold.

Her face was all high cheekbones and lush lips.

Her forehead was high, and her chin was a little pointed, hinting at her stubborn nature.

He'd learned a lot about her in twenty-four hours, and he'd sure never been able to forget her. Six years... That was one hell of a long time for a woman's memory to haunt him. "You still look beautiful," he told her softly.

Her smile flashed again. "Still charming, huh?"

There was no accent to her voice, nothing to give away her roots, but he knew she'd been raised in the South. That bit had been in the dossier he'd been given on her.

He studied her a moment longer, cocking his head. "Why are you here, Jennifer?" He liked the way her name rolled off his tongue.

"I was looking for you."

His brows rose. *You found me.*

She wet her lips and threw a quick, almost nervous glance back at his closed office door. Then she focused on him once more. "I need your help."

Right. Because she hadn't searched for him out of any great, unrequited love.

One night. That's all it had been, for them both.

Besides, most people came to McGuire Securities because they needed help—help getting justice. Help with problems that the police hadn't been able to solve.

He sat on the edge of his desk and motioned to

the chair in front of him. "Why don't you sit down and tell me what's going on?"

Instead of sitting, Jennifer started to pace.

He almost smiled.

"I need protection."

The urge to smile vanished. "From what?"

"Not what—a person." She stopped pacing. Swallowed. "Someone is stalking me. I need you to make sure that this person doesn't get close to me, not again."

Brodie sure as hell didn't like the sound of this situation. "Again?" he prompted. Meaning this person had already gotten to her before?

Jennifer gave a quick nod. For an instant, her expression wavered, and he saw the fear in her eyes. *So it's not gone, after all.* "Three months ago, a man—he attacked me in a New Orleans alley. He stabbed me." Her hand slipped to her right side. Lingered. "I was able to get away from him then."

As soon as she'd said the word *attacked*, Brodie had leaped off his desk.

Her breath sighed out. "But ever since that night, I've had the feeling that someone is watching me. Following me. And last week…my home in the French Quarter was torched."

"You need the cops," he said immediately, the words sharp. "This guy should be in jail."

"He would be, if the cops could find him." Jennifer shook her head and sent her dark hair sliding over her shoulders. "But they can't, and I'm afraid that he'll come for me again." Her fingers slid away from her side. "I'm scared." Her words shook.

He'd clenched his back teeth. With an effort, he managed to grit out, "Your father—"

"Didn't you hear?" She glanced away from him to stare out the window at the city of Austin, Texas. "He died two years ago. A yachting accident."

Hell. "I'm so sorry." He'd lost his own parents in the years since he'd last seen Jennifer. Only their deaths hadn't been an accident—his parents had been murdered.

Their murder was the whole reason that he and his brothers had opened McGuire Securities. The cops hadn't been able to find the killers, but— *We will.* He and his brothers had a new lead on the cold case, and they were finally getting close to delivering justice to the men who'd ripped apart their family.

"My father's company was nearing bankruptcy at the time of his death," Jennifer said as she lifted her chin. "But I promise I have money to pay you. I just…I need your help. You're the only person I can turn to now."

Louisiana's French Quarter and Austin weren't exactly close on the map. "You drove all the way here, just to talk with me?"

Her lashes flickered a bit. "You saved my life before. I was hoping that you could do it again."

He wanted to pull her into his arms. Because he wanted that so badly, Brodie didn't move. "If you need my help, of course I'll take your case."

Her shoulders sagged. "Thank you." Her relief was palpable.

Now he frowned at her. "Did you think I'd turn you away?"

"Three other private investigators have. I went to them right after the fire, but…they said there was nothing to link the two attacks. That it's just random. Really random, terrible luck." She eased closer to him. "But it's not. I know when I'm being hunted."

Brodie nodded. "I'm sure you do." She wasn't the first client he'd seen who'd been turned away by other PIs in the business. Her fear was real, and he'd spend some time investigating to find out just what was happening in her life.

"Thank you."

Those words were too familiar. He'd never wanted her gratitude. On that hot, desperate night, he'd only wanted her. He should have known better than to touch her.

Desire had taken over. He'd never lost control— not before or since that night. Only with her. There was just something about Jennifer Wesley that pushed him to the edge, then *over* that edge.

He glanced toward the clock. It was nearing 7:00 p.m. already. "We can go over the case tonight.

You can tell me everything right now." He'd stay with her until midnight, if that was what it took. "Or we can start fresh first thing in the morning." That would give him time to go ahead and start pulling strings with the New Orleans Police Department so he could get their case files on her attack and the arson at her home.

"Tomorrow…" She hesitated. "That's fine."

He frowned at her. "I can stay here all night if you want."

She flashed him a weak smile. "Tomorrow is fine. I'm actually close to being dead on my feet right now."

His gaze dropped to her feet. Sexy high heels. Delicate ankles. Bright red toenails.

"I drove straight from New Orleans today. After the last PI down there told me he wouldn't take the case, I knew I had to come see you."

How had she even known that he and his brothers had started a PI business? But that wasn't the question he asked, not yet. Instead, Brodie murmured, "You could've called."

Jennifer shook her head. "I thought you were less likely to turn me down in person. And…"

He waited.

"And I needed to get out of that town." Her voice lowered. "I told you, I felt hunted."

Stalked.

But she drew in a bracing breath. "I think starting

fresh tomorrow sounds great. When do you want me here?"

He didn't want her to leave him. Now that she was back, Brodie wanted to keep her close. "How about nine o'clock?"

"Perfect." She turned away. "I'll see you—"

"Do you want to get a bite to eat?"

Her shoulders stiffened, and then she glanced back at him.

Hell. He'd done it again. Why was self-control such an issue with her? "You said you drove straight through, so you must be hungry." He hadn't eaten since lunch, so he was near famished himself. "How about I take you out for dinner, for old times' sake?"

Red filled her cheeks. "Our old times didn't exactly involve dinner."

No, they had involved danger and passion.

The danger was already happening again. As for the passion, well, a guy could dream. "Just dinner," he told her softly. "We both need to eat."

He shut off his computer and headed for the door. No, for Jennifer.

He'd thought about her plenty during the years. Thought that…surely…things couldn't have been as good as he remembered.

He'd also thought that she would have gotten married over the years. In his jealous head, he'd seen her saddled with some rich society boy with more money than sense. Some guy handpicked by her father.

Only her father was dead. And he knew her mother had passed away when Jennifer was just a child.

As she stood before him, Jennifer seemed very much alone.

Not anymore. "You don't have a…boyfriend?"

"No." Her gaze met his. "There's no one like that in my life."

The relief he felt was wrong, and he knew it. So was the thought that he had… *I'm here now.*

In silence, they headed down to the main floor. The elevator ride was pretty close to torture. Mostly because the woman smelled better than sin.

"I heard about your parents." Her confession was hushed.

He lifted a brow.

"Okay, I found out when I did an internet search on you. Brodie, I'm sorry. So sorry for what happened to them."

Yeah, his family's attack had been splashed all over the press in Texas when the murders occurred, and he knew there was still plenty to read about the horror online.

"Did you…did you ever find their killers?"

"We're close," he told her. Closer than they'd ever been before since they'd finally located the weapons used to kill his parents.

Surprise flashed in her eyes for just a moment. "That's great."

The elevator dinged. They stepped into the hallway and her high heels tapped against the gleaming tile. He nodded to the security guard as they left the building and the hot Texas night hit them. His SUV was parked right across the street. He caught her elbow in a light grip and headed for the vehicle.

Just as they hit the middle of that street, bright lights flashed on, locking them in a too-stark illumination. A car's engine revved and tires squealed.

In that instant, Brodie realized the driver of that car was heading straight for him and Jennifer. *Aiming* for them. Jennifer yanked at his arm, as if she was trying to pull him out of harm's way, even as Brodie grabbed tightly to her. They hurtled through the air, dodging that car—a long black car—by inches. The wind seemed to whip around them, and the acrid scent of burning rubber filled Brodie's nose right before he and Jennifer crashed into the asphalt.

The car didn't slow down. It raced to the edge of the street and swung a hard right. The damn thing vanished into the night.

That maniac just tried to kill us!

"See…?" Jennifer's husky voice yanked his stare back to her. She was sprawled right beside him on that asphalt. "I told you… Someone is hunting me."

Not just hunting her. Someone wanted her dead.

"YOU'RE STAYING HERE?"

Okay, so Brodie McGuire wasn't exactly impressed with her choice of lodgings. His tone of voice made that fact loud and clear. Jennifer headed out of the bathroom, a wet cloth pressed to her scratched elbow. That hard contact with the pavement had ripped her skin right off. "Well, seeing as how I had the key to the room and my things are here…" She motioned toward the bed and her one bag. "I'd say that's a yes. I'm staying here." Jennifer tried to put a teasing note in her voice.

But Brodie glared at her. "I expected you to be in a five-star hotel. One with a guard downstairs, making sure that guests were escorted in and out of the place."

Ah, right. He still saw her as Jennifer Wesley, heiress. That was very much the wrong image to have. "There was no money left when my father died." Her words were totally true. Jennifer hated lying to Brodie, so she was trying to stick to the truth as much as possible. "And when my home burned—" *burned, exploded into balls of fire* "—well, it wasn't like I had a whole lot of options available to me." Her luggage bag was filled with clothes that she'd bought during a fast and furious purchase in New Orleans. "I'm trying to save as much money as I can."

Because she was starting to think she might just

need to vanish, and if that happened—cash would be vital for her survival.

"You're on the first floor," he said, a faint line between his dark brows. "The lock on that window is broken." He stabbed a finger toward the left.

The lock was broken? Unease tightened like a knot in her stomach. The lock hadn't been broken when she'd first checked in to the room. She knew because she had double-checked all the locks there.

Brodie's hand dropped back to his side. "Anyone could get in here."

She headed for the window. The lock was smashed all right. *Maybe someone already has been in here.* "I promise that lock was fine earlier."

He swore.

She'd been aware of the furious energy surrounding him ever since that hit-and-run. There'd been no license plate on the car, at least not one that she'd seen, though Brodie had been able to easily identify the car as an older-model Mustang. He'd called the cops and spoken with a Detective Shayne Townsend. Brodie had told her that Shayne was a friend, someone he could count on to help him out with her case.

No uniforms had come out to the scene in order to talk with them, though. Instead, Brodie had bundled her into his vehicle and gotten them away from McGuire Securities.

"Is anything missing?" He pointed to her bag. "You need to check."

Right. She dropped the cloth back in the bathroom and hurried toward her luggage. Jennifer opened up the bag and—

This time, Brodie's curse made her flinch.

Her clothes had been slashed. A black-and-white photo lay on top of the clothes, a photo of her. One that had been taken near the Saint Louis Cathedral in New Orleans.

Someone had used a red marker and written across that photo. Two stark words: *I know.*

She didn't touch the photo. Jennifer knew they could send it to the cops, to that Detective Townsend, and get it checked for fingerprints.

"What does he know?" Brodie asked, voice gruff.

Jennifer backed away from the bag. "I have no idea." She looked up to meet his stare. The rage glittering in his gaze had her sucking in a quick breath. "Brodie—"

"You're coming home with me."

That didn't sound good. Or maybe it did. But she shook her head. "I'll just get a new room. We can turn this over to the cops, and—"

"I'll get Detective Townsend down here with his crime scene team. If the intruder left DNA or fingerprints, he'll find it."

"You…you trust him?" Her experience with cops hadn't exactly been stellar so far. Back in New

Orleans, they'd pretty much thought that she'd had a breakdown after the alley attack, that she was just imagining the stalking.

I'm not imagining anything.

"Shayne Townsend is a friend. We can count on him." He pulled her farther away from the bed. "But you aren't staying here. Your stalker is watching this hotel, watching you, and I'm not just going to leave you alone so he can attack."

The stalker had followed her from New Orleans. Had he been right behind her that entire time? On all those long twisting roads? Goose bumps rose on Jennifer's arms. She'd actually thought that she might be able to just leave the guy behind in New Orleans, but, obviously, she wasn't going to be that lucky.

"You can stay at the family ranch," Brodie told her. "My brothers and I installed the security system there. There is no safer place, and I promise, no one will get to you there."

Her gaze slid back to her luggage. A life shouldn't be destroyed so easily, yet Jennifer felt as if that were exactly what this man was doing to her. Systematically destroying her life.

"There's plenty of space at the ranch," Brodie continued in that deep rumble of his. "So you don't have to worry about me...getting too close."

Just like that, her eyes were back on him.

A muscle flexed in his jaw. "I want you safe. I can keep my hands off you."

She'd never thought otherwise.

"Come with me," Brodie said. "Trust me to protect you."

Brodie McGuire. The years had carved him into an even more dangerous, powerful man. He was big, easily over six foot three, with wide shoulders and a solid build that told her the guy was definitely no stranger to a gym.

He was handsome, almost ridiculously so with that hard, square jaw, that perfect blade of a nose and his green eyes. And the man had dimples. *Dimples.* They flashed when he smiled, and that smile of his made her stomach flip.

He was a threat to her, in so many ways, but he was also the one man who'd never let her down. The one man who could actually keep her alive.

Even if he didn't know all her secrets.

"Come with me," he said again.

She nodded.

JENNIFER WESLEY WAS making a deadly mistake. She thought that an ex-lover could protect her?

She was wrong.

He had her in his sights, and he wasn't about to let her vanish.

There would be no escape. No mercy, either.

He watched as Jennifer and Brodie McGuire left

the run-down hotel. Brodie was right beside Jennifer for every step she took, his body tense, protective.

Jennifer had certainly blinded that man to her true nature.

Brodie needed to be more careful. If he didn't watch it, the ex-SEAL might just find himself targeted, too.

You don't want to die for her.

Because Brodie didn't even really know the woman he was protecting. She wasn't some sweet, lost innocent.

Jennifer Wesley was a cold-blooded killer.

Chapter Two

He had her in his home. Some of the desperate tension that Brodie felt should have eased since they were safe, but it hadn't. If anything, the tension within him just seemed to be growing worse.

He'd called his friend Shayne Townsend again—Brodie and the Austin police detective had been friends for years. He knew he could count on Shayne and his team to search Jennifer's hotel for prints and trace evidence.

He and Jennifer were in the main ranch house. A place that he and his twin brother, Davis, had completely renovated. Sometimes, the house seemed to be filled with ghosts.

And other times, the place felt too damn empty.

Jennifer stood in front of the fireplace, gazing around with wide eyes. The woman had pretty much been through hell in the past twenty-four hours, and she probably just wanted to crash.

He cleared his throat. "The guest bedroom is down the hallway, second door on your right."

Brodie didn't mention that his bedroom was behind the first door on her right. He didn't want to spook Jennifer any more than necessary. *Any more than she already is spooked.*

Her dark gaze slid toward the hallway. "Are we the only ones here?"

He tapped a code in the security panel, making sure that the system was set for the night. "My brother Davis is usually here, but he's working a case in North Carolina right now." Since he and his brothers had formed McGuire Securities a few years ago, their business had started attracting plenty of attention. At first, their cases had primarily been in Texas, but as their reputation had grown, they'd branched out into the South and along the East Coast.

She took a step toward the hallway, then hesitated. "This is going to sound terrible..." Jennifer glanced back at him. "But I'm starving."

Realization slammed into him. *The woman never got her meal!*

"Can I raid your kitchen?" Jennifer asked with a quick smile that made his heart thump in his chest.

He felt like an absolute heel. "I can—I can make you something." Wait, had he just stuttered like some nervous teen? Hell, he had.

The scent of lavender deepened around him as Jennifer eased closer to him. "I don't want to put you to any trouble."

And he had the thought, *Jennifer Wesley is trouble with a capital T.* He caught her hand and led her to the kitchen. Within his grasp, her fingers were soft and silky. Delicate. His hold tightened on her.

The kitchen was cavernous, courtesy of his twin brother's addiction to food. Brodie motioned toward the bar and started rummaging in the fridge. There was plenty of stuff in there that he could use to make her a meal.

"Just a sandwich is fine," Jennifer told him quietly. "After everything that's happened, I'm not even sure I could handle more than that tonight."

He got the sandwiches—one for her and one for his growling stomach—ready in record time. Her smile rocked right through him when he offered the plate to her.

The woman had to be used to dining on meals that were one hundred times better than a ham sandwich, but as they sat together and ate cold sandwiches at his bar, she acted as if she were in heaven.

His gaze kept sliding over her as questions rolled through his mind. The police reports from New Orleans were on their way to him, courtesy of some pull that he had, but there were other answers that only Jennifer could give to him.

Questions he needed to ask her.

She finished her sandwich and flashed him a wide smile.

He hated to make that smile dim, but he had to

ask…"What secret do you have that a man would be willing to kill for?"

He saw it then, the crack in her mask. Fear flashed in her eyes, and her golden skin paled. "I have no secrets."

Her lies sounded just like her truths, but her eyes had given her away. "That's not going to work."

She rose, backed away. "I should get some sleep."

He followed her. "If you want me to help you, then you have to be honest with me." They were back in the den. "What does this guy think he knows about you?"

She didn't look at him. "I have no idea."

"Then start by telling me your secrets. The things that you think no one knows. Tell those secrets to me, and I'll work from there."

Now she did look back over her shoulder at him. He read her hesitation too easily.

"I'll find out," he told her, voice soft, "sooner or later. It's what I do." What she wanted him to do. If Jennifer hadn't wanted the truth to come to light, then she never should have come to his office.

She shouldn't have come back to him.

"What, exactly, are you asking?" Jennifer turned toward him. "If I've committed some sort of crime? Is that what you think happened here? That I did something—and now this guy is after me?"

He had no clue about what she might have done… That was the problem. "You have a man on your trail who wants to hurt you." No, kill her. A knife attack, an arson and a hit-and-run... That wasn't the usual type of stalking case that he heard about. It was one hell of a lot more intense—and deadly. "Do you have a lover that you rejected? A man you turned away who might have—"

"Gone crazy without me?" Jennifer finished as she gave a hard, negative shake of her head. "No, this isn't some rejected suitor."

"Are you sure about that? Because people are good at concealing who they really are. Maybe you thought you were with someone safe, but the truth is...beneath his surface, your lover was as dangerous as they came."

The hardwood floor creaked as she made her way back to him. She stopped, less than a foot away. Close enough to touch. To hold. Her voice was husky and low when she told him, "You're the most dangerous lover that I've had."

Brodie's heart started doing a double-time rhythm as he stared down at her.

"As for secrets..." Her voice as a throaty temptation. "You might be my biggest one. The SEAL I seduced on the night I should have died."

That night was burned in his memory. The desperate raid... Finding her bound and afraid in that dirty room... His job had been to get her to safety while his team provided cover. But the mission had been compromised because they had been given bad intel regarding just how many enemy combatants would be at that location. He'd stolen a Jeep and driven away as gunfire blasted into them.

They'd taken shelter at one of the few safe houses that he knew. And...

"I should have kept my hands off you," he said. She'd been the victim. She hadn't needed him to—

Jennifer laughed. "That wouldn't have worked. Especially since I wanted my hands on you." Her head tilted to the side. "You didn't realize it, did you? How close to death I truly was. They'd left the room moments before you arrived so that they could get ready to kill me. They were going for the weapons...and a video camera. They wanted to record my last moments."

No, she'd been a ransom target—

"I was minutes from death—I knew that. You came in...and changed everything. I wanted to be with you that night because I wanted to celebrate being alive." A small pause, then that soft voice of hers continued. "And I just wanted you, the way I don't think I've ever wanted another man."

That confession was like a punch to his stomach. "Be careful."

Her eyes widened. "Why?"

"Because we're alone here." Miles away from anyone else. "And I still want you, more than I've wanted anyone." The chemistry between them was white-hot. One touch—incineration. He knew the risks, and his body had been far too tuned to hers from the moment she'd walked into his office.

"I…didn't realize." She took a step closer to him.

The woman should be backing away.

His muscles stiffened.

Her dark gaze held his. "If I remember our morning after correctly, you weren't exactly begging me to stay with you."

Because he'd had a job to do. He'd been in the field. The mission waited. He'd needed to thoroughly eliminate any threat to her—that had been the goal. But once he'd left the SEALs…

I looked for you.

He cleared his throat. "Are you sure there isn't another man out there, someone who might have begged you to stay?" *Someone who won't let you go now?*

"There's been no one in the past year."

That revelation surprised him. A woman like her? With those bedroom eyes and sinful lips? She probably had men begging for her affection everywhere she went.

"I've had lovers before," she continued, her voice still husky, "but I hardly think those men would wait so long and then suddenly decide they needed to kill me." And, amazingly, her lips tilted up in one of her slow smiles. "I really do try to only date men who *don't* want to kill me. It's a rule I have."

But she didn't know what was beneath the surface

those men presented to her. Hell, if she knew the darkness that lurked beneath Brodie's surface, then Jennifer would never have let him get close to her.

"I'll give you their names," she said. "But those men aren't after me." Her words held utter certainty.

He thought back to that hit-and-run. Brodie hadn't seen the driver of that Mustang. "When you were attacked in the alley, did you see the man's face?" Maybe that was why she was so sure the stalker couldn't be a former lover.

"He wore a ski mask. He was big, about your size, muscled." Her breath blew out. "Caucasian. I saw his hand—when he stabbed me, I saw the skin near his wrist. He was wearing black gloves but I saw that part of his body."

He waited.

"His body was pressed to mine. His breath on me. I just… You know a lover's body, okay?"

Brodie certainly knew hers.

"You don't forget it. You don't forget a touch." Her breath expelled. "That man isn't a former lover."

Maybe he was someone who wanted to be a lover, but she'd turned him away.

"Brodie, I just want this guy found. I want this mess stopped. I thought my life was finally safe, until he came along."

Finally safe?

She started to turn away but then stopped. "Do you ever wonder... Was it really as good as we remember?"

Her words rocked through him.

Her gaze fell to his mouth. Jennifer's tongue swiped over her lower lip. "It was just the adrenaline, right? The danger? The whole life-or-death situation that we were in. I mean...there's no way that we'd kiss again and—"

"Ignite?"

Her lips parted.

He wanted her mouth. He also wanted to show her that he could be more than the rough SEAL she'd known before, but playing the gentleman wasn't exactly his starring role.

"Yes," she whispered. "Ignite."

Hunger, desire pulsed through him. "You should walk away now."

He'd said words like that to her before. Another time, another place.

She'd been hugging him, her body trembling. He'd tried to do the right thing. Tried to warn her away.

You should walk away.

But she hadn't walked away then. She'd stood on her tiptoes and put her mouth against his.

And now...now she was walking toward him, stopping only when their bodies brushed.

"Are you…are you seeing someone?" she asked as her head tilted back.

"No." The one word sounded like a growl. Mostly because it was.

"Neither am I, but I guess I already told you that, huh?" Her gaze was on his mouth. "It can't be as good as I remember."

How many times had he told himself the same thing?

"One kiss…just to find out?"

Brodie didn't know if he'd be able to stop after one taste of her.

"One kiss…because I don't want to be afraid to-night."

His hands had curled around her waist. He'd pulled her even closer to him. "You should have walked away." Then he did just what they both wanted. What they both needed.

A kiss.

To see if the memories were wrong. To see if that white-hot connection, the electrifying need, could possibly be real…and still there.

He began softly, slowly. His head lowered, and his lips brushed over hers. Her lower lip was full and plump, her top a sensual tease. He kissed her lightly, a brief caress.

Then her lips parted more for him. His tongue swept inside and—

They ignited.

Her hands rose and wrapped around his shoulders. Her nails sank into his skin as she rubbed her body against his. Her tongue met his, her taste drove him to the edge, and the desire he'd tried to keep in check broke through his control.

With a rough growl, he pushed her back against the nearest wall. Brodie caged her there, pinning her with his body. His mouth grew rougher and wilder on hers as the flood of desire deepened within him.

This was the way it had been before. One kiss and nothing else had mattered to him—nothing but taking her, claiming her.

He licked her lower lip, a sensual swipe of his tongue, and she gave a moan that he caught with his mouth. He loved the sounds she made. Loved the way her body rubbed against his.

He loved it even more when she was stretched out before him in bed.

But…

But her hands pushed against his chest.

Brodie forced his head to lift. He stared down at her and watched those long lashes of hers lift.

"It is the same," she whispered.

No, she was wrong. It was even better. The desire even stronger. Brodie knew that he was on the edge of an abyss then, and if he didn't pull back—right at that moment—he'd fall over the edge. And he'd take her with him.

"Why is it this way between us?"

"I—I don't know."

They had a combustible chemistry that was off the charts. He wanted to push her, to get her right back into his bed instead of in the guest room, but…

Some maniac is terrorizing her. She needs safety, not—

Well, not what he wanted to give her.

He sucked in a deep breath, and his hands rose from her. Instead of touching her, Brodie pressed his hands into the wall on either side of Jennifer's body.

"Brodie?"

"Give me a second." Longer than that. Every breath he took tasted of her.

His hands shoved into the wall, and he pushed away from her. Took one step back. Two. "The guest bedroom," he said again, voice gravel rough, "is the second door on the right."

She slipped past him and headed toward the hallway.

"My door—" he shouldn't tell her, but he did, "—is the first one on the right."

The floor creaked, then her high heels tapped as she walked down the hallway. Brodie looked down and saw that his hands had clenched into fists. A door shut—somewhere down that hallway.

He rolled back his shoulders to glance at the clock. It was nearing 1:00 a.m. now. They'd stayed around her hotel room long enough for the cops to arrive—then they'd been grilled by the uniforms Shayne had sent over.

Jennifer needed to crash, and so did he.

But instead of sleeping, he sure would rather be tangled in the sheets with her as they let the adrenaline and desire churn through them both.

Brodie waited a few more moments. Then he turned out the lights in the den. He marched toward the hallway to that first door on the right. He opened the door slowly, aware that he was holding his breath. But...

Jennifer wasn't in his bed.

His breath expelled in a rush. *Hell.* Maybe he'd be taking a cold shower before he crashed.

JENNIFER HEARD BRODIE'S door open, then close. Her heart was racing so fast that she thought it might burst right out of her chest.

Did he realize that she'd almost gone into his bedroom? Her draw to Brodie was too strong. She hadn't counted on that. Desire was supposed to be easy to control, but when she was with Brodie, her mind and body couldn't seem to remember that important fact.

She just reacted when he was near.

Glancing around the room, Jennifer's attention fell on the big bed. A heavy wrought-iron bed. She stripped but kept on her underwear and bra since she hadn't exactly come equipped with pajamas.

Jennifer climbed in bed and pulled the covers up to her chin. The ranch house creaked a bit around her, and the wind howled as it hit the windows.

Brodie's home. A place of joy for him, and a place of incredible sorrow. She'd done her research before running to him—she'd needed to be sure the SEAL she'd known before hadn't changed over the years.

He *had* changed, though. He'd become harder, and now, sadness flickered within his gaze, a sadness that seemed to haunt him. Oh, he did a good job of wearing his mask, of pretending to have no emotions, but she could see right through his facade.

Maybe it was easy for her because she was so used to wearing a mask of her own.

She knew that his parents had died in this house. They'd been murdered, shortly after her own rescue by Brodie in the Middle East. If the accounts she'd read online were true, Brodie's younger sister had been at the ranch during the attack, but she'd escaped.

Some folks thought that his sister, Ava, wasn't just an innocent victim.

They thought she might just be a vicious killer.

The pipes rattled a bit, and she could hear the thunder of water coming from the room next door. She had a sudden flash of Brodie in the shower.

Jennifer swallowed. Getting involved with him again should not be on her agenda. If he found out the truth she'd been keeping from him, then any personal involvement would just make him feel more betrayed.

She didn't want that. Brodie McGuire was her safe port in this storm. A man with an impeccable record, and a man with deadly killing skills.

Before this nightmare was over, she might just need those skills.

Brodie had been very wrong when he'd asked if a former lover was the one after her. The few lovers she'd had in the past didn't know her secrets. This man—this man who hunted her so relentlessly, he did.

I know. The picture in her luggage wasn't just some random shot. It had been taken right after her last meeting with her government contact. Taken on the day when she'd finally bid farewell to a life that wasn't really hers.

She'd always feared that life might destroy her, but Jennifer had never expected that destruction to come just when she was finally free of the thick web of lies that had twined around her for so long.

But freedom had a cost in her business, and that cost… It might just be her life.

A FAINT SOUND woke Jennifer hours later. Her eyes flew open just as she heard the creak of her door's hinges.

Someone was coming into her room.

"Brodie?" Her voice was soft, uncertain. She

yanked the covers up to her chest. It was so dark in the room, and her eyes were frantically trying to adjust. She could barely make out a large looming shadow in the doorway.

The shadow was roughly as big as Brodie, because his shoulders seemed to stretch and fill that doorway but…"Brodie?" she said again.

Jennifer was pretty sure the shadow shook its head.

He found me. And if her stalker had gotten through the security at the ranch, what had he done to Brodie? Fury and fear pumped through her as she jumped from the bed. Jennifer grabbed for the lamp on the nightstand. She didn't waste time screaming. She threw that lamp right at the shadow that was now staggering toward her.

The man swore as the lamp hit him, but he tossed it aside. The lamp shattered when it crashed into the floor. Even as that lamp smashed into a hundred pieces, Jennifer was already launching herself at her attacker. She went in fast and hard, just as she'd been trained, going for his weak spots. Right for the eyes with her thumbs even as her knee aimed for his groin.

But the shadow had been trained, too. He grabbed her, swearing, and he shoved her up against the nearest wall. Her head immediately rammed toward him as she tried to break his nose.

"Jennifer!" That roar came just as the lights in the room flashed on.

Jennifer froze, her head bare millimeters from her target. Her gaze jerked to the door. Brodie stood there, clad in a pair of jeans, his chest heaving, his eyes glaring—at the man who held her in a too-tight grip.

"What the hell is happening?" Brodie demanded as he rushed into the room. "Davis, get your hands off her!"

Davis? Her gaze jerked back to her attacker and Jennifer's breath caught in her throat. The man she was staring up at—he had Brodie's face. Brodie's unforgettable eyes.

"Just trying to stop her from ripping off my head," the man—Davis—muttered.

Davis's hair was a little longer than Brodie's, and, though their eye color was the exact same, Davis looked…harder, rougher than Brodie. There was something there, a darkness that lingered in the depths of his eyes.

"If I let you go…" Davis drawled, his Texas accent a bit more pronounced than Brodie's, "do you promise not to throw another lamp at me?"

She wasn't going to make a promise she couldn't keep. "How about you just promise not to try sneaking into my room during the middle of the night?"

"Davis." Brodie grabbed his brother's arm and yanked him away from Jennifer. "Why are you in here? With her?" He took up a protective position right next to Jennifer.

Davis rolled his shoulders and exhaled on a long sigh. "I've been up for over thirty hours, bro. I just got in town an hour ago. I stumbled home, and all I wanted to do was crash."

"Your room," Brodie snapped, "is on the other side of the house."

Jennifer glanced over at Davis once more, and she found his gaze sliding over her body. Appreciation was in his stare. "The view on this side of the house is much better."

Swearing, Brodie put his body in front of hers. "She's not an option for you. Forget that *now*. Go find *your* room. Crash there and make sure you stay away from her."

Jennifer craned her head and saw Davis put his hands up as he backed away. "Easy. I didn't realize you had a girlfriend spending the night."

Brodie stiffened. "She's not my girlfriend."

For some reason, those words stung a bit. But he was right. She wasn't his girlfriend. *Former lover?* Was he about to reveal—

"She's a client, and she's here so she can have protection, not so she can be terrified by you in the middle of the night."

Davis stopped his retreat. "I didn't know." His voice was a rumble. "Sorry, ma'am. Didn't mean to scare you."

Her breath rushed out. "I…" *What?* "It's fine," she mumbled.

"Go, Davis," Brodie ordered.

Davis went, but he did cast one last look back at them, a guarded, measuring glance, before he left the room.

When the door shut behind Davis, Brodie whirled toward her. "I'm sorry. My twin brother can be— hell, difficult."

"I…I didn't realize you two were identical twins." For some reason, she hadn't expected to find a carbon copy of Brodie at that ranch. Fraternal twins, sure. *Why* had she thought that? When she'd been researching Brodie, she'd come across a reference to his twin, but she hadn't thought the guy was his identical match.

"We're only alike on the outside." He flashed her a grin, and his dimples winked. "I'm the easygoing twin."

Was she really supposed to believe that? There wasn't a whole lot that was "easy" about the former SEAL standing in front of her.

Brodie's gaze dropped to her body.

Her pretty much unclothed body.

A muscle jerked in his jaw, right before he spun around, presenting her with the broad expanse of his back.

She hurried to grab her shirt. Jennifer went to yank it on and—

Brodie lifted her up into his arms. "Be careful," he whispered. "You almost cut yourself."

The shattered lamp.

He carried her back toward the bed. Eased her to her feet. But didn't let her go.

She should tell him to let go.

She *really* shouldn't enjoy his touch so much.

"I wanted you to feel safe here." His voice seemed to vibrate around her. "I'm sorry that my brother frightened you. It won't happen again." He dropped his hold and stepped back. "I'll clean up the mess and—"

Her hand caught his. "Do you know what scared me the most?"

He looked at her hand wrapped around his wrist, and then his gaze slowly rose to her face.

Her lips pressed together; then she admitted, "I knew that…in order to get to me, my stalker would have to take you out first. I was afraid he'd hurt you."

When she'd decided to seek out Brodie, she hadn't thought of the danger that she'd put him in. She'd been selfish, too scared, and now Jennifer had to face the ramifications of what she'd done.

His hand lifted and curved under her chin. "I'm an ex-SEAL. I can take care of myself."

Then his lips brushed against hers. The kiss seemed bittersweet. She found herself leaning toward him, wanting to just hold him tight and sink into him.

I should have stayed away. But when a woman had no options, she tended to act desperately.

His lips rose from hers. "You'll always be safe with me," he promised her. Then he turned away.

She believed he meant those words. Deep at his core, Brodie was the true-hero type. She'd known that…counted on it.

But…

Would he always be safe with her?

BRODIE PULLED THE guest room door shut behind him. He paused a minute, his mind still on Jennifer.

And on ripping his brother's head off.

"I thought you'd stay in there longer." Davis's voice came from just down the hallway.

Brodie glared at his brother. "Shouldn't you be crashing somewhere?" Somewhere on the *other* side of the house.

Davis's eyes slid back to the closed door. "She really a client?"

She was more than that.

"Because I saw the way you looked at her, and I also saw how close you were to swinging a punch at me."

Davis had been drinking her in with his eyes. Everyone thought that Brodie was the one with the love-em-and-leave-em reputation. They didn't know the truth. Davis was the one who could seduce so easily. "She's not for you," Brodie said flatly even as his hands clenched into fists.

Davis cocked his head to the side. "If she's for you, then why are you out here with me? Instead of being back in that room with the woman *your* eyes seemed to be devouring?"

Because he was trying not to scare the woman. Brodie closed the distance between him and his brother. "Someone is stalking her. Terrifying her. *Our* job—" and, yeah, he stressed the *our* because everyone at McGuire Securities would be working to keep Jennifer safe "—is to protect her."

Davis gave a slow nod. "You know you can count on me."

He did. He knew that his brother would have his back, always. The man might infuriate him, but Davis was the one person he trusted above all others in the world.

They'd weathered the storm of their parents' death together. They'd trained as SEALs together. No one knew him better than Davis did.

Davis knew just about all his secrets. Except…

I never told him about Jennifer.

"That woman has training," Davis murmured. "She almost took me down."

Not an easy feat, considering the number of times that Brodie had sparred with his brother.

"She was seconds away from gouging my eyes out and breaking my nose," Davis added.

Brodie's brows climbed at that news. Jennifer had always struck him as delicate, almost breakable.

"She didn't even scream." Davis had turned away and was wearily walking down the hallway. "Just attacked. Got to admire a woman with a fire like that."

Yeah, you did.

He glanced back at Jennifer's closed door.

But where had a high-society girl like Jennifer learned to fight so well that she'd almost taken out a man with SEAL training?

It seemed that Jennifer might have more secrets than he'd realized. Thoughtful now, Brodie returned to his room and booted up his computer. When Brodie checked his email, he saw that the case notes from the New Orleans attacks had been sent to him. Eyes narrowing, he began to read...

THE SECURITY AT the McGuire ranch was good, too good. The McGuires had been determined to turn their home into a fortress after their parents' death, and they'd sure succeeded in that plan.

In the darkness, he searched for any weaknesses that would allow him access to his prey. He searched, but he found none.

He made sure not to trigger any alarms. After all, he wasn't an amateur.

If he couldn't get to Jennifer, because she was secured so tightly on the McGuire homestead, then he'd just have to rip that safety net away for her.

Maybe it was time for Brodie McGuire to realize that Jennifer was a serious threat, one that shouldn't be anywhere near the other members of his family.

Jennifer couldn't be trusted, and she *shouldn't* be protected because, at her core, she was just a killer.

How long will it take before you throw her to the wolves, Brodie McGuire?

He couldn't wait to find out.

Chapter Three

Jennifer wasn't going back to sleep. Not then.

Not with fear and adrenaline pumping through her, not with her emotions all twisted and her body too tense.

Not with her mind focused so much on Brodie.

He didn't understand what he meant to her. In the darkest moment of her life, he'd been there. A savior she hadn't expected.

Jennifer slid from her bed. The shards of the broken lamp had been swept away and her footsteps made no sound as she headed toward the door.

She fully realized that she could be making a huge mistake, but Jennifer didn't care. She wasn't going to play it safe this time. Not with him.

She tiptoed into the hallway, turned toward the room next to her own and lifted her hand, poised to knock. After drawing in a deep breath and attempting to control the faint trembling of her fingers, Jennifer rapped lightly on his door.

A few seconds later, that door was yanked open.

"Look, Davis, I'm not talking about—" Brodie broke off, his eyes widening as he focused on her. "Jennifer? What's wrong?" Then his hands closed around her shoulders and he shifted her a bit to the side as he looked behind her. "Is my jerk of a brother bothering you again? I *told* Davis to back off."

Jennifer shook her head. "I needed to see you."

Surprise rippled over his face.

She didn't want to have this conversation in the hallway. Not where Davis might pop up again. "Can we go in your room?"

He backed up. She advanced. He shut the door behind her and flipped the lock.

His brows shot up at the soft click. A lamp near his bedside had been turned on, and the light cast a soft glow over his bed and his tangled sheets. "Jennifer?"

"I can't get to sleep."

"Join the club," he muttered, running a rough hand through his hair. "But, um, you don't want to be in here with me right now."

"I don't?" This was exactly where she wanted to be.

His hand dropped. "You look really good in that shirt."

She glanced down at herself. After he'd run Davis out of the guest bedroom, Brodie had brought her a shirt to sleep in—one of his US Navy shirts. It fell to her knees, seemed to swallow her.

It smelled liked him. Maybe that was why she hadn't been able to get him out of her head.

Or maybe there were other reasons.

"Go back to your room, Jennifer." His voice was low, hard.

She didn't move. "You asked me before…why the connection was this way between us." She'd wondered about it, too. Why they touched and truly seemed to ignite.

But maybe they shouldn't question the connection. Maybe they should just enjoy it. Life was short and brutal, and moments of perfect pleasure were too rare.

"I want you," she told him, the words a soft confession. "When we touch, when we kiss…" Her voice faded away. She didn't even know how to explain her feelings.

He walked toward her. His hand lifted and cupped her chin.

And she realized that she didn't have to explain. His eyes were bright with the same passion she felt.

Her fear began to fade away. He had a way of doing that. Of making the danger seem less—of making her feel so safe.

"I want you," he said, giving her back the same words she'd just spoken to him.

Then his head lowered, and his mouth took hers. The kiss was soft at first, slow and caressing. As if he was afraid of frightening her. But she wasn't afraid of his desire or of her own.

Her hands curled around his shoulders. Her mouth pressed harder to his, and just like that— they ignited.

Need ripped through her body. Her heart thundered in her chest. She couldn't get close enough to him. Her nails bit into his skin, even as her body pressed tightly to his.

A growl built in his throat. Then he was lifting her up, holding her easily in his arms. His mouth didn't leave hers. He kept kissing her, and the desire inside Jennifer wound tighter and tighter.

He took a few steps, then lowered her onto the bed. The soft mattress dipped beneath her. Brodie eased back a bit. He stripped the shirt off her and tossed it across the room. She still wore her bra and panties, and his gaze slowly slid over her body. His eyes were bright with desire, and his stare lingered on her breasts. Her hips.

"You are so beautiful."

He made her feel that way.

His fingers eased under her body, and he unhooked her bra. She was pretty sure he tossed it somewhere, too, but Jennifer wasn't exactly paying attention. His mouth was on her breast. His tongue stroked her, and her body arched off the bed toward him as a dark desire surged through her.

His hand eased down her stomach. Touching,

caressing. And he kept kissing her breasts. Stroking her with his mouth and tongue until Jennifer thought she'd go out of her mind.

"Brodie!" Right after she called out his name, Jennifer bit her lip, worried that she'd been too loud, worried Davis might hear them.

Brodie's head lifted. "I like it when you say my name like that." His hand flattened on her stomach. "Davis is on the other side of the ranch house. He can't hear you. Every sound you make...it's all for me."

He began to kiss his way down her stomach, then he paused, his mouth hovering over the scar on her right side. The knife wound.

"I'll find the SOB," Brodie promised, and he pressed a kiss to that scar. "He won't ever hurt you again."

His tenderness caught her off guard. She'd expected the storm of passion, but that gentleness? Jennifer wasn't sure how to handle that care. He made her feel uncertain, vulnerable.

Her hands slid down his chest. Down, down, until she found the button on his jeans. She popped open that button and eased down his zipper.

His hands closed around hers.

"I don't want to wait," Jennifer told him, her voice husky. "I need you. *Now.*"

There was too much darkness in her life. She needed the wild rush that Brodie could give to her.

He pulled away her panties. She shoved down his jeans. Brodie spent a few moments taking care of the protection for them; then he was back, settling between her thighs.

Her legs wrapped around him, and he thrust into her. Her breath caught then as her gaze locked with his. She wanted to freeze that one moment in time, to hold it close to her heart, to remember it always.

Passion and pleasure…to protect her from the fear.

But he was withdrawing, thrusting again, and the rhythm grew out of control as they raced toward release.

She'd thought the pleasure they'd shared before had been good.

She'd been wrong. This was beyond good. Beyond anything she'd felt before.

When the climax hit her, the waves seemed to consume her whole body. Brodie stiffened and whispered her name. Then he was kissing her. She could taste his pleasure and her own, and she never, ever wanted the moment to end.

Pleasure shouldn't be fleeting. It should last longer than the pain.

Pain is always with me.

Aftershocks trembled through her. Her body quivered.

Then his head lifted. He smiled at her. Such a

tender, sensual smile on the face of a man who was so dangerous.

His lips brushed over hers, and the pleasure began to build again.

JENNIFER PICKED UP her shirt from the floor. She looked back over her shoulder, but Brodie hadn't stirred on the bed. Part of her—a very big part—wanted to stay with him. To still be in his arms when the sun rose.

But she was afraid that she might have given too much of herself to Brodie during those hot, wicked hours. Jennifer felt vulnerable, lost, and she needed time to get her guard in place again.

When she left the room, Jennifer tried to be as quiet as possible. In the hallway, the floorboards creaked beneath her feet, and she froze, but there was no sound from Brodie's room. Breathing slowly, carefully, she made her way into the room she'd been given.

Jennifer shut the guest room door, then leaned back against the wooden frame.

A tear slipped down her cheek. Sometimes, it was so hard to remember that she couldn't have the things other women possessed.

Like a lover who cherishes me.

Because none of her lovers had ever known who she really was. They'd just seen an image she presented. None of her friends knew who she was. *No one* knew the real woman hiding behind the mask.

Sometimes, Jennifer wondered if she even knew herself.

WHEN HE HEARD the creak of the floor, Brodie's eyes opened.

She'd run from him.

Just when he thought that Jennifer was letting him get close. Two steps forward…fifty back.

He rolled over. The bed smelled of her. Sweet lavender. And he could still feel her against him. Silken skin.

Jennifer could run for now. It wasn't like she'd get far, not while he had her in his house and under his protection.

SUNLIGHT TRICKLED THROUGH her window. The day had finally dawned. A soft knock sounded at Jennifer's door. She'd been awake for a while, lying in that bed, staring up at the ceiling and wondering just how much she should reveal to Brodie. After last night, she knew things would be different between them. He'd expect answers. He'd deserve them.

When she heard the knock, Jennifer hurriedly pulled on her clothes and rushed to the door. She took a deep, fortifying breath and opened the door. *My mask is back in place.*

"Morning," Brodie's voice was low, and his stare seemed guarded.

Jennifer tried to offer him a tentative smile. "Good morning." The words came out way too husky. She just couldn't look at him without remembering what they'd done last night. She was sore in spots because of what they'd done.

He lifted some clothing toward her. "I, uh, I figured you'd want some fresh clothes."

He had extra women's clothes just lying around his place? She didn't exactly grab for the offered goodies. What very well could have been jealousy began to burn within her. She'd thought what they had together was special, but maybe to him—

"They're my sister's," Brodie explained. "Ava doesn't come around much, so I don't think she'll mind you borrowing them. You two seem to be about the same size so…" He shrugged. "I just thought you'd like them. But if you don't want the clothes—"

"I do!" She'd much rather wear fresh clothes than the bloody and torn things she had on. And since the offering he'd brought her didn't belong to some random woman who'd spent the night at the ranch…Jennifer grabbed the clothing. "Thank you."

His stare sharpened on her. He opened his mouth, but then stopped.

What do you want to say? Tell me, Brodie.

Jennifer waited. A thousand words were flying through her own mind right then, but she didn't know where to begin.

He took a step back. "The bathroom's down the hall. You can shower, then meet Davis and me for breakfast."

Davis. Right.

Were they even going to talk about last night? Maybe they shouldn't. Maybe it was for the best.

The morning after wasn't exactly her best scene. Perhaps they would just pretend that the sensual hours hadn't happened.

"It was better than before."

Jennifer almost missed those rumbling words. Heat stained her cheeks. "Yes." It had been.

"I'll want more…of you."

She wanted more of him. That was her problem. Jennifer was afraid she'd always want him, and she couldn't blame that desire on an adrenaline rush or on a danger high or anything else like that—not this time.

She simply wanted him.

He was a weakness that could prove lethal for her.

"You came to me last night…"

She hadn't been able to stay away.

"You *will* come to me again, and when you do, I'll be waiting."

She looked into his eyes, and saw the sensual promise there.

Definitely lethal.

She started to close the door, but his hand flew up, and his fingers curled around the side of the door frame, halting her movement.

"One more thing…"

"Brodie?" Something in his expression put her on guard.

"I want you like hell on fire. We need to both be clear about that. I look at you, and I need. I want."

Her breath came faster.

"But I can also tell you're keeping secrets."

Secrets were her life.

His head cocked as he studied her. "You wouldn't lie to me, would you, Jennifer?"

She had, and she would again. There were some things that she would never be cleared to tell him. "Why would you ask me that?" He'd gone from making her heart race with desire to making her tremble in fear. She didn't want him getting too close to the truth about her.

She feared if he found out the truth, Brodie would turn her away. Jennifer couldn't let that happen because he was her last hope.

"I'm starting to realize there's a lot more to you than just meets the eye." He studied her with an assessing stare. "You need to tell me your secrets."

She shook her head but then caught herself.

Brodie's suspicious gaze said he'd caught the telling movement. "You *will* tell me, or I'll discover them on my own."

He let the door shut and she heard his footsteps march away.

"YOU'VE BEEN HOLDING out on me," Davis accused him.

Brodie lifted his brows as he entered the kitchen. He wasn't the one holding back. *That's Jennifer.*

"Now that I'm not running on fumes, want to tell me the real story about the looker staying at our ranch? You know, the woman with a body to beg for and near-ninja skills?"

Brodie downed a cup of coffee. "Her name's Jennifer Wesley, and you need to keep your damn eyes off her body."

Davis narrowed the eyes in question. "Why is her name familiar? I swear I've heard it before."

That was a fairly easy question to answer. "Because her father used to be an oil magnate, before his company went broke and he decided it was better to die at sea than to face his creditors." He'd been digging into her past that morning. After she'd left him, sleep sure hadn't come again, so he'd spent more time on his computer.

Davis exhaled on a long sigh. "The guy just left his daughter to face all that alone?"

"From all accounts, yes."

Davis rubbed a hand over his jaw. "And where

do you fit into the picture that is Ms. Wesley? Because I might've been tired, but I saw the way you looked at her last night."

"Just how did I look at her?" And if he brought up that crap about wanting to devour Jennifer—

Well, Davis would be right.

"Like a lover. Like she was *your* lover."

She was. Brodie glanced over his shoulder, toward the doorway. Jennifer wasn't heading toward them, not yet. "She's our client, that's what we need to focus on now."

"But *before* she was a client? I mean, just how did the lovely Ms. Wesley know about our security services?"

She knew because she'd tracked him down. His fingers tightened around his coffee mug. "I was on a rescue mission once... A wealthy American's daughter had been taken hostage in the Middle East. My job was to get her out alive. I did." He kept the details of that time as brief and emotionless as could be. Davis would understand exactly what he was saying and what he wasn't.

"You saved her once, so she came to you for help again?"

Something like that. Brodie put down the coffee mug.

The floor creaked. He glanced back at the doorway once more and saw Jennifer standing there, her hair still wet, her face free of makeup. And she was so beautiful. He actually found himself taking a step toward her before he forced his body to be still.

"I think I'm bigger than your sister." She glanced down at her body. The tight jeans fit her like a perfect glove.

"Looks good to me," Davis muttered as he came to Brodie's side.

Brodie elbowed the guy. He'd warned Davis about keeping his eyes off Jennifer's body.

Jennifer nibbled on her lower lip. "Are you sure she won't mind me using her clothes?"

It was Davis who replied. "Ava doesn't come here." He glanced around the room. "She can't see any good memories here anymore. Only death."

Sadness flashed across Jennifer's face. "I'm sorry."

So was he. While he'd been halfway across the world, his parents had been slaughtered, and he still didn't know why. But after years of dead-end leads, they'd finally recovered some solid evidence recently. They'd found the guns that had been used to kill his parents. The guns had been hidden inside an abandoned cabin, an old cabin that bordered their ranch's property.

"What's the plan for today?" Jennifer glanced, rather nervously, toward the window. "As much as I'd like to keep hiding here, that's not an option that will last forever."

No, it wasn't.

"If he doesn't already know I'm here, he will soon. He followed me from New Orleans. He found my hotel room." She swallowed. "He'll find me here, too, and I don't want that threat coming down on you and your family. You've already suffered enough."

"I read the reports from the NOPD."

Her eyelashes flickered a bit.

"You fought off the man who attacked you in that alley. According to the police, you said that you broke his nose and were able to escape from him."

Her shoulders moved in a slight shrug. "I told them I *thought* I'd broken his nose. I mean, it sounded like those bones crunched."

His brows rose. "And when the fire started, sweetheart, you failed to mention that you were *in* your house." That detail had enraged him. He kept picturing flames rushing toward her delicate skin. "You climbed out a second-story window and scaled down the side of your house in order to escape."

Davis whistled. "Nice."

"No," she said softly. "It was actually rather terrifying. The trellis I used to climb down was old and it was breaking beneath me. Crumbling with every move I made. I was afraid it wouldn't last long enough for me to reach safety."

His eyes closed. *Too close.*

"I don't understand what's happening here," Jennifer said, anger roughening her words. "I mean, are you grilling me *because* I've managed to survive for so long? Was I supposed to let the guy kill me?"

No. His eyes opened. "The arson was deliberately set—judging by the report, a professional was at work." A guy who'd known exactly how to set a fire for ultimate destruction capabilities. "And the attack in the alley? That was an isolated spot, a timed attack." Something that was nagging at him... "The guy stabbed you in the side and managed not to even hit one major organ."

"Lucky for me," she murmured.

His gut told him something more sinister. "Maybe it was lucky because the man knew exactly what he was doing."

Silence.

Maybe he wanted to hurt you, but not kill you. Not then. Had the guy been just playing with her in that alley?

Davis glanced between them. "You think some kind of hired killer has targeted her? Why would someone like that be after a society girl?"

She shuddered.

"Why indeed?" Brodie murmured. Because now that he'd learned more details about the attacks, he was sure thinking the stalker wasn't some ex-lover who'd been scorned. Maybe Jennifer had been right to deny that claim. When he'd seen the arson reports, his suspicions had sharpened. This wasn't some enraged maniac coming after her.

They were looking at a controlled, organized killer. But *why* was that killer after Jennifer?

"If you aren't honest with me," Brodie told her flatly, "then we're going to have a problem." He couldn't work in the dark.

She backed up a step.

"What does the man after you *know*?" He couldn't forget that photo and those two words that had been written across it.

"I have no idea." Her voice was wooden.

He hated having to interrogate her. She'd come to him for help, so why was she holding back? Why was she making him push her? "The picture was taken at the Saint Louis Cathedral in New Orleans." He'd recognized the spot because he'd handled a few cases in the Big Easy. "What were you doing when that picture was taken?"

"I was…just going for a walk."

Lie.

His stare cut to Davis. His brother's expression had tightened.

"We can't help you—" Brodie forced the words between his teeth "—if we don't know what we're up against."

Her gaze fell to the floor. "You didn't know what you were up against in the Middle East. When you rushed in to save me, you had no clue how many men would be holding me. You came inside anyway."

Because that had been the mission. Save her, at

all costs. And he *had* thought that he'd known what he was facing. Too late, he'd learned their intel was wrong. "Jennifer—"

His phone started to ring. Brodie yanked it out of his back pocket, then frowned when he stared down at the screen. He didn't recognize that number. He was tempted to ignore the call, but...

It could be another client—someone in a desperate situation who needed him.

And Jennifer was filling a plate with eggs, giving him her back.

Huffing out a breath, he answered the call. "Mc-Guire."

"She's lying to you." The voice was a low whisper. *"Don't believe the things that she says."*

"Who the hell is this?"

"Her father didn't commit suicide and it was no boating accident..."

His attention was locked on Jennifer's back.

"She killed him."

Jennifer?

"She's using you. Setting you up."

Brodie unclenched his jaw to say, "I'm coming after you." He knew he was talking to Jennifer's stalker. "I'm going to find you, and I'm going to make sure you get locked in a cage."

Jennifer whirled toward him, her eyes wide.

"Why don't you ask sweet Jennifer what she

knows about the murder of your parents? Why she knows her way around your ranch so well?"

"Look, you son of a—"

The line went dead.

"Brodie?" Jennifer put down her plate and crept toward him.

He immediately tried to do a redial on the jerk. But the phone rang and rang. *Hell, no.* So Brodie tried another option. He got his brother Mac on the line. Mackenzie "Mac" McGuire had connections that they could use. "Mac, listen—no, damn it, I don't care if you're half awake. I need you to run a trace on a telephone number." He rattled off the number. "I have to know who this guy is, and I need to know *now*."

He hung up the phone. The fury rushing through him was so great that his hands were shaking, and he balled them into fists. That fool had brought up his family. His *family.*

"That was him?" Jennifer asked, and her hand touched his shoulder. "He called you?"

Brodie gave a curt nod. "He's trying to turn me against you." Like he didn't recognize the oldest trick in the book. He recognized it all right, and it infuriated him. "Giving me some bull about you killing your father—"

Her gaze cut away from his.

"And you knowing intel about my parents' death." Of course, she didn't know anything. Why would a society girl from Louisiana know about the murder of two Texas ranchers?

Davis stalked toward them. "He said that crap to you?"

Brodie's stare was on Jennifer. She'd paled. And she wasn't meeting his stare.

"Jennifer...*he was lying, wasn't he?*" Brodie demanded.

His phone rang then, but this time he recognized Mac's number. He put the phone to his ear. "Tell me you found out who—"

"The phone belongs to a Jennifer Wesley," Mac said. "You know who that is?"

He was staring right at her. "Yeah, I do."

"Don't ask about the strings I pulled—"

He tried never to ask.

"But I got a buddy to try and locate that phone. I figured it had to be working since you called and woke me up at helluva-too-early o'clock."

Despite the tense situation, Brodie's lips almost twitched.

"He triangulated the signal, and the caller is close."

"How close?"

"Within ten miles of the ranch."

He followed us.

"Do you need me?" Mac demanded. "Because I can be on my way in two minutes."

"I got this." He wasn't about to let the stalker play his games, not on Brodie's home turf. "Thanks."

"Anytime…"

He pushed the phone back into his pocket. Jennifer was watching him with wide eyes. "When you escaped that fire, did you leave your phone behind?" Brodie asked.

She nodded.

"He's got it." He marched for the door. "And the guy is out there right now, playing with us." He planned to find the man. The stalker would have taken to shelter, trying to stay hidden as he attempted to monitor what was happening at the ranch. "Stay here," he threw over his shoulder as he hurried out. "I'm taking him down."

He left the main ranch house and headed for the stables. If the stalker was watching the main road that led to the ranch, then Brodie sure didn't want to advertise his presence as he hunted. And the best way to do that?

Sneak up on the guy. He went into the stables and started saddling his horse.

When he heard the tap of soft footsteps behind him, Brodie whirled around and found Jennifer standing just a few feet away.

"You're going after him?" she asked.

He grabbed the reins for his horse. "Damn straight."

She crossed to him. "He's that close? You're sure?"

Close enough to watch them, but the stalker hadn't set off any of the alarms that protected the perimeter of the ranch. Not yet. "He won't see me coming," Brodie assured her. That was why he planned to take his horse. The guy would be looking for a car, not a rider on horseback. "Not until it's too late."

Her gaze slid over the row of stalls in the stables. "I'm coming with you."

The hell she was. "Stay with Davis. He'll keep you safe."

She was already marching toward the nearest stall. "This man has been terrorizing me for months. I'm not just going to stand back while you go after him by yourself. I won't risk you just to save myself."

What—she was his backup? "Can you even ride a horse?" He blurted the question out before he had the sense to stop himself.

Her head jerked toward him. Her eyes became angry slits. "Betting I ride better than you, cowboy." Her voice had turned arctic. He watched as she expertly saddled her horse and then leaped into the saddle.

Well, well. Wasn't she full of surprises? "My mistake," he muttered.

Her father didn't commit suicide...and it was no boating accident...

She killed him.

"Brodie?"

He checked his weapon. If he had her close, then he could be sure Jennifer was safe at every moment. "Stay behind me the whole time, understand?"

She nodded.

"Then let's go get him."

As THEY NEARED the northwest side of his property, Brodie slowed his horse. He wanted to go in softly as he approached his prey. Lifting his right hand, he signaled to Jennifer that they needed to be careful.

If Brodie were going to hide out and watch the ranch, if he were looking for a perfect vantage point that would provide him protection from prying eyes, he would pick the spot about twenty feet to the right. It was the spot that a trained hunter would choose, a man used to stalking prey.

That's why I'm out here. I think that SOB is too much like me.

Not just your average perp, but a man who knew far too much about hunting human prey…and killing.

Brodie tied his horse to a tree and watched Jennifer do the same. As they crept toward the fence, he pulled out his phone. He knew this particular area always had good cell reception—and he'd been counting on that for his plan. There had been a reason why he left Davis behind—and that reason wasn't just because his brother hated riding horses.

"Cut the security system," he told Davis when his brother answered. "Give me ten seconds." Because he had to get past the fence and he didn't want any alarms announcing his intentions.

"Start counting," Brodie told him.

Ten, nine...

Brodie grabbed Jennifer's hand, and they cleared the area. Then Brodie kept them in the trees as much as he could as they advanced. One step, two and—

He saw the edge of a long black car. The Mustang that had tried to run them over the night before.

Got you. A cold smile curled Brodie's lips as he advanced. The stalker had cut across the property located immediately next to the ranch. His car was there, half-concealed in the shadow of the trees. Brodie approached the car cautiously. He searched the scene, but he didn't see any sign of the person who'd made the call to him.

Jennifer's steps were silent behind him.

He peered through the car's window and saw a phone on the seat. A phone and a manila envelope. Brodie's name was scrawled on that envelope.

You knew I'd come looking for you.

And what? The guy thought he'd just jerk open that door and retrieve the envelope? Brodie was no fool. That car could be wired. As soon as the door opened—*boom*.

"Where is he?" Jennifer's body pressed to

Brodie's. Her whisper in his ear was a bare breath of sound. "I don't like this."

Neither did he. The guy had wanted them to come out there and find him. Hell, no wonder tracking the phone had been so easy.

"What's in the car?" Jennifer asked, voice low. She tried to peer inside.

His gaze was on the trees to the right. Brodie thought he'd just glimpsed a light from those trees, as if metal had glinted when the sunlight hit it.

"Back away," Brodie said softly to Jennifer.

"What?"

His instincts were screaming at him. He grabbed her and yanked her to the other side of the car just as gunshots rang out. The bullets missed them as they ran, but the shots peppered into the side of the Mustang.

Then he heard the roar of an engine. Brodie looked up just as a motorcycle burst through the trees. Lifting his own weapon, Brodie aimed for that vehicle. He fired off a shot, and he knew he'd found his target when he heard a hard grunt.

But the driver didn't fall off his bike. He revved the engine and raced away even as he kept firing back at Brodie.

Dirt swirled in the motorcycle's wake. Brodie ran after the bike, but he wasn't about to catch up to the guy driving. "Damn it!"

"Brodie?" Jennifer's voice was hesitant behind him.

He grabbed for his phone to call his brother. "Davis, the guy is heading north. He's on a motorcycle, and he's armed."

"On my way," Davis told him instantly. Brodie knew that Davis would try to intersect the guy, provided the man stayed *on* the road. Since he had a motorcycle at his disposal, there was no guarantee the stalker would stick to any of the main roads in the area. The slippery SOB might escape from them again.

He whirled around, looking for Jennifer, and he saw her reaching for the Mustang's door. "Jennifer, don't!"

But she already had the door open. She grabbed inside for the envelope, and he grabbed her. Brodie jerked her back, holding her tightly against him. "What are you doing? That thing could be wired to blow!" It still *could* blow. He hauled her with him, running back toward the trees and—

The Mustang exploded.

H E BRAKED THE motorcycle when he heard the explosion. *Just had to go for the file, didn't you?*

His hand rose and pressed to his left shoulder. McGuire had hit him, and the bullet had driven right through his flesh. But he was used to the pain. After what Jennifer had done to him, a bullet wound was *nothing*.

He'd stitch that wound up himself once he was

clear. Another scar to join the others that marked his body. Another wound that *she* would pay for.

His bloody fingers curved around the handlebars. A glance over his shoulder showed him the billowing black smoke that was rising into the air.

I need to make sure she's gone.

He wasn't about to leave Jennifer's death to chance. He drove the motorcycle back toward that smoke. He saw the wreckage. The flames.

But no blood. No bodies. No sign of Jennifer or her hero at all.

Chapter Four

"You could have been killed!"

Brodie had finally stopped their mad, frantic race away from the flames. They were back near the horses, and the animals neighed when they saw Brodie.

He grabbed her arm, his grip tight and his face angry. She tensed. "The car was wired to explode," Brodie snapped. "If you had lingered inside for just a few seconds more—"

"I'd be dead," Jennifer finished as her breath heaved out. "Right, I get it." He didn't need to scare her with what-if scenarios, since she was already pretty terrified as it was.

His gaze fell to her hand and the manila envelope that she clutched. "You really think whatever is in there—you think it was worth dying for?" Before she could answer, he shook his head. "I didn't think I'd get to you in time."

"Brodie—"

"I was afraid." His words were whispered now,

but his eyes were still bright with fury. "In my mind, I saw you dying right in front of me."

Then he kissed her. It wasn't a soft, light kiss. It was a kiss of desperation. Passionate. Wild with need.

She leaned toward him and kissed him back just as fervently. She'd been afraid—for him—when those bullets started flying.

"Don't scare me like that again," Brodie whispered against her lips as his head rose a bit. "Don't."

Jennifer couldn't give him a promise that she might not be able to keep.

He drew a ragged breath. His mouth came toward hers again. She rose up, leaned into him—

And he yanked the envelope right from her hand. *No!* "Brodie—"

He ripped open the envelope. A black-and-white photograph spilled out. As soon as she saw the image, Jennifer knew her carefully constructed world was about to fall apart.

Because it was an image of her, an image that had been taken years ago. She was standing beside Brodie's mother, standing right outside the McGuire ranch house.

She knew exactly when that image must have been snapped. Because despite what Brodie believed, she *had* visited the McGuire ranch in the past.

She'd been there…days before both of Brodie's parents had been killed.

His fingers whitened around the picture. "It's a fake." His voice was a hoarse rasp, one that she barely recognized.

There was so much pain on his face.

She wouldn't lie to him—couldn't lie, not then.

"It's a fake," he said again, but this time his gaze flew up to meet hers.

Jennifer shook her head. "No, it's not."

Shock came first, then anger. Betrayal. "What is going on?" Brodie demanded.

Seeing that picture, knowing that she'd been tracked to the home of Brodie's parents, Jennifer just couldn't keep up the lies. Not when he'd been seconds away from dying. *Because he was saving me.* "I'm not who you think I am."

"I'm figuring that out."

But he was learning the truth...too late.

FOUR ANGRY MCGUIRE men glared at Jennifer. She was back at the McGuire Securities office. Davis hadn't seen any sign of the man on the motorcycle. He and Brodie had searched the area, but they'd turned up nothing.

And then they'd taken her in for questioning.
Like I'm the criminal.

Maybe...maybe she was.

Grant McGuire was seated behind his desk. From her research, she already knew he was the eldest McGuire brother. His eyes raked over her, and his face was a stone mask. Grant was the former army ranger. The one who'd first formed McGuire Securities after he'd left the military. From what she'd learned about Grant, the man was a force to be reckoned with and definitely not someone you'd want as an enemy.

It's a pity he seems to be my enemy now.

Mackenzie "Mac" McGuire stood to the right of Grant. He was the one who'd been in Delta Force. When he spoke, his voice was clipped, hard. He looked like the other McGuires—same green eyes, same handsome but hard features. Same glare at her.

Davis and Brodie were to the left of Grant. Brodie was glaring at her, and Davis, well, he kept casting nervous glances at his twin.

She felt rather nervous when she looked at Brodie, too.

"Ms. Wesley," Grant's voice was smooth, totally lacking emotion. "There's a date and time stamp on this image."

Yes, unfortunately, there was.

"You visited our parents just days before their death. That was a visit that none of us were aware of."

That had rather been the point. Secret visits were supposed to be *secret*.

"Why?" Brodie rasped. "Why did you see them?"

She took a bracing breath. The *why* was actually

easy enough. The rest of the story would be the gut-wrenching part. "Because you saved me."

His brows shot up. "What?"

"You risked your life to save mine. After what you did for me, did you honestly think I'd walk away without trying to repay you?" *I always pay my debts.* Her gaze slid to the picture. Brodie's mother had been a lovely woman. Kind and friendly. And Brodie had gotten his dimples from her.

"How did you even find my mother?" Brodie stalked around the desk and came toward her. "You only had my first name. You wouldn't have been given clearance to a SEAL's files."

"I have more clearance than you know." Her clearance was a big part of the problem. Her hands tightened around the arms of her chair. "You risked your life for me. I just wanted to…to show you I was grateful. I found your parents. I offered them—"

"Money?" Davis supplied.

"Yes." Because money had been all that she could offer them. She'd been paid well for the work that she'd done over the years, so she'd wanted to give that money to someone who deserved it.

"How much?" Brodie gritted out.

"Fifty thousand dollars."

His eyes widened. "And my parents took the money?"

"Not at first." At first, his mother had been shocked. She'd been adamant that her son had just been doing his job. But… "Something changed. I was only in town for two days. I told her to call me if she changed her mind. I tried to convince her to keep the money. She could use it for the ranch. For her retirement. Something." And she wouldn't feel so guilty for the risks Brodie had taken. "An hour before I was scheduled to leave, she called me at my hotel. She wanted the money, but she needed it to be in cash."

Brodie's brows climbed. "I'm supposed to believe that?"

"It's true!"

"My mom didn't need money! The ranch was fine. My brothers and I—we always sent her money. She wouldn't take that kind of cash from a stranger."

A desperate woman will do anything. The last time she'd seen Brodie's mother, nervous tension had clung to the woman.

"I got her the cash. I delivered it to her at the ranch." Her gaze slid to the photograph on the desk. "That's when that image must have been taken. The bag in her hand? That's what I put the cash in."

He whirled back toward the photo. Silence filled that room, stretching uncomfortably.

When Jennifer lifted her gaze, she found Grant staring straight at her with an unreadable gaze.

"Do you know who killed our parents?" Grant asked her, his voice quiet.

Jennifer shook her head. "I didn't even find out

they were dead until…until a few months ago."
When her stalker had appeared. When she'd realized there was a very short list of people who could help her, people she could trust.

Brodie had been at the top of that list.

So she'd started researching her onetime hero, and then she'd learned about the tragedy that had wrecked his family.

After she'd given the money to Brodie's mother, Jennifer had left Austin and been flown straight to Paris. Another assignment waited, and she hadn't been able to look back.

If she had…could she have changed the fate of Brodie's parents? Even since seeing that black-and-white photo, a new fear had risen within Jennifer. Had they died because of her? Had she taken danger right to them?

"I didn't make the connection between their deaths and me," Jennifer whispered. "Not until I saw the photograph. I didn't think anyone knew what I'd done. I tried to be so careful." Her heart hurt in her chest. If she was truly the cause of all the pain that Brodie had been through, when she'd just wanted to help him…

"Why would you need to be careful?" This time, it was Mac who spoke as he stepped forward. He'd been so still before, but she'd been aware of a wild intensity that seemed to cling to him. His eyes—a shade lighter than Brodie's—narrowed on her.

"Who cares if a society princess visits a ranch in Texas? Why would that matter to anyone?"

If she had been just a society princess, then it wouldn't have mattered. Her gaze sought Brodie's. This was the moment she'd dreaded. "I'm not who you think I am."

He closed the distance between them once more and seemed to surround her. "Tell me something I haven't already figured out."

He stared at her as if she were a stranger. To him, she probably was.

Sometimes, I feel like a stranger to myself. "When you found me in that little room…when my captors took me, I wasn't being held because someone wanted to ransom me." The breath that she inhaled seemed to chill her lungs. "I was being held because someone had found out that I was working undercover for the US government. My cover was blown, and they were going to kill me."

Brodie shook his head. "No, your father—"

"Nate. Nate Wesley." She said his name softly as she pictured him in her mind, dressed in his expensive suit, a gold ring flashing on his pinkie finger. Oh, but he'd been perfect in the role of her father. "I've never been a society princess, but I was picked to play that part. Just as Nate was picked to play the role of an oil magnate." She smiled at him, and the smile felt sad on her lips. "All intel isn't gathered on the battlefield. Sometimes, secrets are shared in boardrooms and ballrooms. A cover was made for me. A cover was made for the man who acted as my father. We were given missions to complete, jobs to do." And they'd done them. Again and again.

Jennifer nervously wet her lips. "After you rescued me, I had one job to complete in Paris. I did it, and I got out of the business."

"Spies don't just get out of the business." Grant was studying her with calculation. "It's never that easy."

A spy. Yes, for all intents and purposes, she'd been a spy. "Nate and I were expected to be in certain circles. Certain wealthy, connected circles. If you lose your wealth, well, to the people who moved in that world, you *were* dead. They immediately cut you from their lives. To get out of that cover...reports were leaked that Nate was losing his wealth." Only Nate had wanted to carry things one step further. He'd wanted to sever all ties to his former life. "Then he had the...accident...on his boat."

"I'll be damned." Mac paced to the window. "Is he even dead?"

She wasn't about to reveal any more intel on Nate. He had a new life somewhere. A new wife. She wasn't going to draw him back into this nightmare.

"The man on the phone..." Brodie's voice was low and hard. "He said you killed your father."

"He's wrong."

"Or you're lying," he threw right back.

Jennifer flinched, but she'd expected his attack. His rage was palpable. *I knew he'd feel betrayed.* The last thing she'd wanted to do was hurt him.

"I mean, you've lied to me before, right? So how do I know you're not lying right now?"

Their gazes locked. He was leaning over, so close that she could see the flecks of gold hidden in the green of his eyes.

"Why did you even seek me out?" Brodie demanded. "Are you being stalked or is this some giant setup? Hell…that hit-and-run, the gunshots today—they were aimed at me, not you, weren't they?"

What? Was Brodie seriously suggesting that she was somehow setting him up to die? She put her hands against his chest and shoved back. "Stop it!" She jumped to her feet.

But Brodie blocked her path before she could storm away. "Why did you come to find me?"

"Because you were the only one I could trust!" Jennifer basically yelled her confession at him. "I'm not in the business any longer. That means I'm pretty much dead and buried to the government contacts I had before. The whole deny-all-knowledge bit, I'm sure you've heard of it. And the friends I made back then? When I was the oil magnate's daughter? How fast do you think they vanished when word got out that the business was broke?"

A muscle jerked in his jaw.

"You saved me before. You risked your life. You showed me that you could handle dangerous situations. I believed that I could trust you." He hadn't been working a secret agenda. She had. "When my back was against the wall, I needed someone I could depend on to help me. I thought that person was you." Her spine straightened. "But I guess I was wrong. I'm sorry I bothered you. You won't be seeing me again."

She turned from him and took two steps. Before she could take a third, his arms wrapped around her and he pulled her back against the hard expanse of his chest. "You don't get to vanish that easily." His words were a whisper against her ear, and she recognized them for the threat that they were.

Her eyes squeezed shut. "I don't know anything about your parents' death. I can't help you."

When he turned her in his arms, Jennifer forced her eyes to open.

"What happened to the fifty grand?"

"I don't know."

"Why did they need the money?"

He could ask those questions all day long, but her answer would still be the same. "I don't know. I didn't question your mother. I just gave her the money and left."

He stared at her as if she were a stranger. *I'm not, Brodie, I'm not!*

"If I knew, I would tell you. Do you honestly think I'd lie to protect some killer?"

When he didn't answer but just stared back at her, Jennifer's eyes darkened even more with her own growing fury. "For years, I worked to protect people. I risked my life to put criminals away— criminals who dealt in arms trades, drugs. I put everything I had into my job." Until she'd felt there was nothing left of her to give. "I would never protect a killer."

He had no clue about what her life had been like. By the time he'd burst into that little room, she'd been playing the role of Jennifer Wesley for so long that she didn't know how to be anyone else. She'd felt hollowed out, empty.

And she'd been moments away from her own death.

Then Brodie had appeared. He'd offered her escape. Life. A second chance.

Behind Brodie, Grant cleared his throat. "You came to McGuire Securities because you had a stalker after you."

There was no past tense. The guy was *still* chasing her down. The near death by explosion she'd experienced that morning should be proof of that.

"'I know,'" Brodie whispered. He shook his head. "That's what he meant by that picture, right? The guy knows you aren't really Jennifer Wesley. He knows what you did for the government."

She was afraid that he did.

Brodie's hold tightened on her. "He took the picture of you at the ranch years ago. If he was following you then, that maniac could be the one who killed our parents."

"Brodie, I'm—"

He yanked his hands back, as if she'd burned him. "If he saw you pay them fifty grand, then he could have thought they were working with you. That they were involved in your undercover missions. The hit on them always looked professional."

Mac swore.

Her gaze flew around the room, and she saw that Davis had frozen—no, his body had frozen, but his eyes were blazing with emotion.

"The man watching you could have killed them because he thought they had intel on *you*."

She hated the torment in his voice. "If all of this is true…then why didn't he come after me sooner? If he wanted me dead for all these years, then why did he wait?"

His eyes glittered. "I guess that's a question we'll have to ask the SOB…when we catch him."

SHE WAS BACK at the ranch, only this time, Jennifer sure wasn't feeling like a welcome guest. Grant and his brothers had grilled her for most of the day. She'd told them as much as she could without revealing classified information.

She knew Grant was using some of his government contacts to try and corroborate her story. She'd tried to tell him that he'd get no corroboration. She'd been too deep undercover to have official records at the government agencies.

Denial is the only rule they'll follow.

Nervous energy hummed through her as she paced in front of the fireplace. Brodie had been so distant with her. And she didn't blame him. She'd known that when the truth came out, he'd turn from her.

So she'd grabbed tightly to him last night. Taken the pleasure and let the fear go.

That fear was back with a vicious force now.

"I'm heading out."

She whirled toward him. She hadn't even heard the guy approach.

"The police are done with their crime scene analysis at the bomb site, and they found nothing." His hands were clenched at his sides. "I'm going for a look myself. They could have overlooked something, and if they did, I'll find it."

Her chin lifted. "I'm coming with you."

"Jennifer—"

"Give me a weapon, and I can guard your back. I'm far from helpless."

"I never thought you were. I wouldn't make that mistake."

His words dug into her like bullets. "I want to catch this guy just as badly as you do."

He held her gaze.

"I'm coming with you," she said again, and, after a hesitation that lasted too long, he finally gave a grim nod.

They didn't talk on the way to the stables. As soon as she walked in, the scent of fresh hay hit her. The horses neighed at her approach. She brought her mare forward, the same horse she'd ridden before, and the black beauty bumped her nose against Jennifer.

"Lady," Brodie muttered. "Her name's Lady. She used to be Ava's horse, until Ava got so terrified of this place that she couldn't come home."

Jennifer stroked Lady's mane.

"Ava was only sixteen when she came home and saw our parents' murder. She told me…Ava thought they were going to kill her, too, but she ran away. Managed to make it to the Montgomery ranch— they're our only neighbors within miles out here." He ran a hand through his hair. "When the cops couldn't find any leads, gossip started spreading that Ava wasn't a victim. That she'd been in on the killings all along."

Her heart ached for him—for Ava.

"We're going to prove that Ava is innocent. And the people who killed my family—they're going to spend the rest of their lives in prison, if they don't get the death penalty."

He took out his own horse, controlling the steed easily. The sun was starting to set as they made their way out of the stables. Streaks of orange and gold shot across the sky. Jennifer stopped, her breath caught by the gorgeous sight.

"Ava can't see the beauty here any longer," Brodie said, his voice sad. "All she sees is the blood and the death."

Jennifer's gaze slid away from the sky and locked on him. "What do you see?"

He wasn't looking at the setting sun. He was looking at her. "Dreams that were lost."

Her heart seemed to stop.

"This was my safe haven. Whenever I'd come back from my missions, my tours, I knew this place would be here for me, waiting. No matter what hell I faced, my refuge was waiting for me."

Until that refuge had been ripped away.

"Davis and I...we rebuilt the main ranch house. We didn't want Ava to walk in and see—" He broke off, clearing his throat. "We tried to keep the good memories and get rid of the bad ones, but it just didn't work."

She hurt for him and all that he'd lost. "Maybe you should try making some new memories."

He gave a grim nod even as his eyes raked over her. "Is that what you're doing? Trying to give up the life you had before and start somewhere new?"

"I didn't really have a life before I became Jennifer Wesley." She hadn't meant to say that. Jennifer jumped on her horse. "We don't have a lot of daylight left. We'd better hurry."

"Jennifer…"

Her mare rushed forward under Jennifer's guidance. She'd bared enough of her soul that day.

THERE WAS YELLOW police tape still up at the scene of the explosion. Brodie secured his horse and walked forward cautiously. The ground was blackened, and every time he thought about how close Jennifer had come to death—

He forced himself to take a deep breath. *She's alive.*

She was also a very, very good liar.

"I want to scout around the woods, see if this guy left any other tracks." He studied the scene around him. The stalker had driven out there on an old dirt road. He'd left the Mustang, setting it up as the perfect bait.

Then he'd waited…just waited for them to follow the signal from that phone.

Boom.

"The cops traced the motorcycle's tracks to the main road, but the guy vanished there." Either he'd kept going on the bike, hitting old trails and dirt roads, or he'd had another vehicle waiting for him.

It would have been a simple matter to load the bike into a truck or a van and then vanish.

A simple matter…especially since they were dealing with a professional. A man who seemed to particularly enjoy fire. *First her house, now the car.*

What would be next?

Brodie figured the guy had stuck to the old trails. Davis had set up a watch position near the main road, but he hadn't seen the guy on the motorcycle come roaring through. Not after the explosion.

"Stay close," Brodie ordered Jennifer. If the guy had come back, he could be hunting them at that very moment.

He wanted to find the man. If that jerk had been responsible for killing Brodie's parents…

I swear I will make him pay.

He'd learned to track at an early age, but when Brodie slipped into the woods near that old dirt road, he didn't see any signs of his prey. Branches weren't broken, and the earth wasn't disturbed. No footprints had been left behind.

He kept searching, fanning out. Jennifer was silent as she followed him.

Guarding his back, just as she'd promised.

The sun sank deeper into the sky. The gold vanished, and the streaks of red started to look more like blood.

But still he found no trace of the stalker.

The guy is good.

That fact made him exceptionally dangerous.

"Nothing," Brodie snapped when they went back to the horses. "The guy is a ghost."

Jennifer's gaze swept the area. "Ghosts can't hurt you. It's only the living who can do that."

She reached for her horse's reins, but Brodie's hand flew out, and he caught her wrist.

"Why did you come to my bedroom last night?" Because he was starting to think that the woman was playing him, pulling him into some kind of game that he didn't understand. He wanted to trust her, but she'd been lying to him from the start.

"Because I wanted you." She was staring down at his hand, and his fingers tightened around her wrist. "I was tired of feeling afraid. When I'm with you, you push the fear away, at least for a little while."

"Jennifer…" Then it hit him. *Is that even her name?* He dropped her wrist and stepped back. "What's your name?"

Her head jerked up.

"Jennifer," Brodie snapped out. "She's just pretend. A cover. What's your real name?"

She flinched, and what could have been guilt knifed through him because he saw the pain in her eyes. *She's been lying to you. You have to protect yourself. Protect your family.*

And you have to use her to find your parents' killers.

"Jennifer is my real name," she whispered. "It's easier…in the business…if you keep things simple. Keep your first name the same or close to your real one. You're already used to answering to that name. Seems more natural." Her gaze slid away from his. "Wesley isn't the last name I was born with, but I've had it for so long that…well, the other name doesn't matter anymore."

She climbed onto the horse. He wasn't about to let this go, not yet. "What about your family? Your *real* family. Do you ever see them?"

Her hand slid into the horse's mane as she leaned forward. "I don't have a family, Brodie. I spent most of my teen years bouncing from one foster home to another." She gave a slow nod. "That's one of the reasons I was recruited, you see. It's better not to have close ties with anyone."

Better?

"They gave me the option of dying."

"What?" Shock punched him in the gut.

"I could have started with a brand-new identity, someplace else. But I thought I was safe as Jennifer Wesley. No one knew the truth about me. No one outside of my division was supposed to know." She drew in a shuddering breath. "I guess I was wrong about that."

The sun had fallen even deeper into the sky. Jennifer shivered.

Get her in for the night. In case that maniac is out there, watching, waiting...

"Want to hear something ridiculous?"

He mounted his horse, then frowned at her.

"You knew Jennifer Wesley. If I became someone else..." Her smile was bittersweet. "Someone with a new face and a new name, then it would be as if we'd never met before." She shook her head. "I didn't want to lose that. I didn't want to lose everything again."

Then her horse rushed by him. He stared after her a moment as her words replayed in his head. Part of him was furious with her for her deception. But another part...

As if we'd never met...

Another part was determined to keep Jennifer as close as he possibly could. Brodie spurred his horse after her.

HIS PLAN HADN'T WORKED.

Brodie hadn't turned on Jennifer. He hadn't kicked her out, hadn't left her to face the wolves on her own.

He'd seen the picture, but the fool must have chosen to believe whatever lies she'd spun.

Jennifer Wesley was very skilled when it came to

lying. After all, he'd believed her lies, too—every word that came from her sweet lips.

Then he'd been captured, tossed into a cell, and forgotten.

Did you really think you wouldn't have to answer for your sins against me?

He'd had eyes on her, even when they'd been an ocean away. And now that he was killing close, there truly would be no escape.

He wondered if Jennifer realized he'd just been playing with her so far, drawing out the kill.

In that alley, he'd just had to spill first blood. It was the way the game always started.

Then he'd started that fire at her home, a carefully timed explosion, but he'd known she would escape. The fire wasn't set to kill. *It was set to destroy your safe haven.*

The hit-and-run outside McGuire Securities? That had been just a little taunt to let her know he was close.

He'd set the bomb in the Mustang with a time delay. He'd wanted her to get out of the vehicle and wanted Brodie McGuire to see the photograph. That image should have made Brodie cast her aside.

Then he would have moved in for the kill. Jennifer Wesley's death would be an intimate event. He'd take her far away from the rest of world. It would be just the two of them, for days…until he ended her suffering. And he *would* make her suffer, just as she'd made him endure years of torture.

Jennifer Wesley's past had come back to haunt her.

You reap what you sow.

Time to up the stakes.

Chapter Five

She'd taken care of her horse. Lady was settled for the night, and Jennifer was ready to crash. She turned away from the stables, her shoulders slumping and her steps slow with a sudden weariness.

Why can't the danger ever be over? I wanted to leave that life behind me.

"I don't trust you."

She stumbled to a stop at that low, rumbling voice. A voice that was very similar to Brodie's but...

It belonged to his twin. The harder, rougher drawl gave him away.

Jennifer glanced toward the shadows of the ranch house and saw Davis. He'd been so still that she hadn't noticed him when she'd left the stables. He'd blended perfectly with the growing darkness.

It was a mistake that Jennifer shouldn't have made. Being a civilian had made her soft. She'd stopped looking for threats in every corner.

Davis stepped away from the house and advanced toward her. "I don't trust you," he said again. "And, unlike my brother, I'm not so tangled up in you that I can't see the danger you present."

Brodie was tangled up in her? Since when? She glanced over her shoulder. Brodie was still in the stables, settling down his horse.

Davis caught her arm, and her attention snapped back toward him. "No one is going to hurt my brother."

"I'm not here to hurt him." Hurting Brodie had never been part of her plan.

"Aren't you?"

She tried to search his gaze, but it was too dark for her to see much at all. But she could feel the deadly intensity that clung to him. "The last thing I want to do is hurt Brodie." That was the truth.

He pulled her toward him. "My brother was almost run down the first night you came to town. Today, he was seconds away from being blown to hell and back."

She swallowed.

"There's a target on you. By coming to my brother for help, you put a target on him, too."

Tears stung her eyes. Brodie had been her only hope. She'd actually thought her stalker would stay behind in Louisiana, that she'd buy time by going to Brodie and that—

No, I didn't think this through. I was scared and I fled. I never thought about the risk to Brodie.

"Help me to get away," Jennifer whispered.

His hold tightened on her.

"I don't want him hurt," she said, and she fought to keep the emotion from her voice. "I don't want any of you hurt." Especially since it appeared she'd already led pain to the McGuires before. *Dear God, did I cause their parents' death?* Ever since she'd seen the picture her stalker had left behind, the question had haunted her. "Distract Brodie, give me a car to use, and I'll vanish."

Vanishing… Hadn't that been her backup plan all along? But she'd been so determined to cling to this life she had. A life that had never been her own, not really.

It's time to let go.

Because when it came down to a choice…letting Jennifer Wesley live or protecting Brodie… Well, there was no choice.

The stable doors groaned behind her. She knew the sound meant Brodie was coming out. "Help me," she told Davis, making sure her voice wouldn't carry far. "Tonight…distract him, and I'll vanish."

Gravel crunched beneath Brodie's booted feet. "Everything all right out here?"

This time, the Texas drawl was stronger in his voice.

"Everything's fine," Jennifer rushed to reassure him.

"Davis?" Brodie closed in on them. "There a reason why you're holding her arm?"

And Davis did still have his grip on Jennifer.

He dropped her arm, fast, and backed up a step.

"I stumbled," Jennifer said quickly. She didn't want Davis lying to his brother. She was the one good at lying, so why not stick with her skill set? "Davis steadied me."

"Did he?" Brodie's voice was doubtful.

She forced her shoulders to straighten. "I'm too tired. Barely walking straight. I think I'll just…turn in for the night."

No, she thought she'd plan her escape. As she passed him, her gaze cut to Davis. She still couldn't read the expression in his eyes, but he gave an almost imperceptible nod.

Relief made her feel a little dizzy. He was going to do it. She'd slip away. Brodie would be safe.

And Jennifer Wesley would vanish.

BRODIE WATCHED JENNIFER as she headed into the house. Her shoulders were stiff and her stride too fast.

"That woman is trouble."

The door shut behind Jennifer, and Brodie glanced at his brother. "That woman is the key to finding out what happened to our parents."

A few weeks back, they'd finally found the guns used to murder their parents. The weapons had been hidden beneath the floor of an abandoned cabin—an old cabin that was just miles from their ranch. All those years, the murder weapons had been close, practically under their noses, and they'd never realized it.

The guns had proved to be a ballistics match for the crime, but there had been no prints on the weapons. The men who'd broken into their parents' house that long-ago night—Ava had said that they'd worn black ski masks over their faces.

They didn't know the identities of the killers, but they would. The McGuires wouldn't stop until they'd gotten justice.

"You think our parents were killed because of Jennifer?" Davis asked him quietly.

He sucked in a deep breath. "For years, I thought they died because of one of us." It was a dark truth that had eaten away at him for too long.

Davis backed up a step.

"You, me, Grant, Mac, even Sullivan…we were all working different black-ops missions back then. One right after the other." Because all the McGuire brothers had left the ranch and went right out and gotten lost in danger. Once, Brodie had craved that rush of adrenaline. As a SEAL, he'd always been walking on the edge of death; he'd known that.

But he'd thought the risk was his alone. Until he'd realized that his enemies could follow him home.

"I thought," Brodie continued, "someone wanted payback because of what we'd done. That our parents were caught in the cross fire because of us."

He still believed that. Hell, even if Jennifer's enemies had tracked her to the ranch house in Austin, wasn't that still on Brodie's shoulders? He'd been the tie to Jennifer. His parents' death—

"I thought the same thing." Davis's voice was low. "The guilt never stops, does it? They were always there for us, but when they needed our help, when we could have saved them…"

They'd all been too far away.

Brodie's gaze swung back to the house. "Whoever is after her…that guy was here, taking pictures, days before our parents died. Either he was here his own damn self or he had some flunky doing his dirty work. Maybe her stalker is the one who killed them. Or maybe he saw who did. Either way, I will find that man, and I will make him talk." Two men had been there the night Brodie's parents were murdered. The stalker and his flunky? Or someone else?

Brodie marched toward the house.

"She's planning to leave."

He swung back around to face Davis.

"She wants me to help her vanish, and I…I gave her the impression I would."

He stalked right back toward his brother as fury pumped through him. "Want to tell me why the hell you'd do that?" *Jennifer can't vanish. I won't let her. I…need her.*

"Yeah, I'll tell you." Davis rolled back his shoulders and stood toe to toe with Brodie. "Because you keep getting caught in the cross fire when she's around. I lost my parents. I don't want to lose my brother, too."

"You're *not* helping her," Brodie snarled, fighting to keep his fury in check. How could Davis not see the danger? "If she leaves, she's dead."

Davis shook his head. "Only if we aren't keeping an eye on her. Maybe she leaves, and that sicko out there thinks she's easy pickings. If he goes for her, then we move in on them both." Davis's words came out in a rapid-fire burst. "And when we do that, maybe we'll finally close in on the people who ripped our lives apart."

"You want her to be bait." He had to unclench his back teeth in order to force those words out.

Davis didn't deny the charge. "You got a better idea? I mean, you could always try nearly getting blown to bits again for her, because, you know, that worked out so well for you before."

His hands were fisted, and it took all his self-control not to take a swing at his twin right then.

"We'd have eyes on her," Davis continued quickly, as if sensing how close to the edge Brodie might be. "It's not like she's a civilian. That woman has training. Let's use it. Let's—"

He grabbed Davis by the shirtfront and jerked his brother toward him. "I'm not using her!" His words blasted out. "So come up with a new plan!"

Did Davis really think he'd just put Jennifer at

risk? She'd nearly been *blown to bits*, too. Every time he closed his eyes, he saw that explosion, only in his mind he hadn't pulled her back quickly enough. She'd screamed for him, and then the world had erupted.

"She is our best plan." Davis's voice was soft.

Brodie's hands fisted in Davis's shirt. "She's not yours to risk." He shoved him back.

Davis swore. "You're too caught up in her."

He turned away from his brother. He wasn't going to argue on this point. Jennifer wouldn't be put at risk like that. End of damn discussion.

"Why?" Davis called after him. "Why won't you even consider that this could work?"

"Because she can't be hurt!"

The lies that she'd told…yeah, he felt the burn of that betrayal. He wouldn't be trusting her again. But Davis didn't get it.

I can't risk her.

He pounded up the steps and shoved open the door. He was aware of Davis following behind him, but he didn't slow down. He hurried down the hallway and turned toward that second door on the right.

Brodie didn't waste time knocking. He grabbed the knob, turned it—

Locked.

"Jennifer!" His fist pounded into the door.

She didn't answer.

Has she already left? "Jennifer!"

Still no response.

So he kicked in that door.

But the room was empty. He ran inside, looking around, searching for her—*gone.*

He rushed back through the house and nearly knocked Davis to the floor. "She's gone!"

Davis's eyes widened. "No...she can't be—"

She's gone. "Were you supposed to keep me out there, keep me talking, while she vanished?"

Davis swallowed quickly. "I was going to distract you, but not yet. She would need a ride to get off the ranch and she doesn't—"

Davis just didn't seem to understand how determined Jennifer could be. Brodie pushed his brother to the side and ran for the garage. Jennifer didn't need them to give her car keys. The woman's whole life was a lie—so Brodie was betting that she knew plenty of handy tricks that would surprise most folks.

Tricks like taking a security system off-line.

The alarm hadn't sounded when she fled the ranch house, and he'd damn well bet the woman went out one of her bedroom windows.

Tricks like hot-wiring a car.

He ran into the garage and saw a shadow moving inside his SUV. Brodie flew toward that vehicle. He yanked open the driver's-side door.

Jennifer didn't even cry out in surprise. She was

crouched under the dashboard, her hands working feverishly with the wires. Her head turned slowly toward him.

"Uh, hi there, Brodie…" Jennifer mumbled.

Davis burst into the garage.

Brodie tried to get a stranglehold on his fury. "Going somewhere?" he demanded.

"Um, no." Her fingers pulled away from the wires. She sat up, rolling her shoulders a bit.

"Jennifer…" Her name was a warning.

"I…might have been going for a little ride."

Davis hit the lights, and illumination flooded the garage.

Jennifer took one look at Brodie's face and winced. Then her eyes locked on Davis. "I thought you agreed to keep him busy," she snapped.

Brodie fired back, saying, "You *both* thought wrong."

Her fingers tapped against the wheel.

She looked so damn cute and sexy right then… and he was *furious* with the woman.

"You walk away from me," he gritted out, "and you're a dead woman."

Jennifer inhaled a sharp breath.

"You came to me because you needed help." His hands were fisted as he fought the urge to grab her and hold on to her as tightly as he could. "Now you're running?"

Her gaze rose to meet his. "Now I'm trying to

protect you because it seems…" She gave a sad shake of her head. "It's seems I may have already hurt you enough."

He stared straight into her eyes. "Leave."

She blinked. "I, uh, was trying to—"

No, sweetheart, you're not going any place. "Davis, get out of here now," he ordered without glancing at his brother. "I'll deal with you later."

"Brodie…" Davis wasn't leaving. Brodie could tell by the sound of his footsteps that his brother was coming closer. "I was going to watch her. I was going to—"

He spun toward his brother. "She wasn't going to wait for you to follow her! She was going to vanish. She was either going to rush right into a trap that stalker has for her out there or she was just going to disappear completely. Become someone new, someplace new." How could his brother not see that?

Davis's eyes narrowed. "I just want to help you."

"Leave us alone, bro. Just leave us alone."

Davis gave a curt nod and shuffled back. He stopped near the exit and glared at Jennifer. "*Not* the plan."

Then he was gone.

Silence.

Brodie tried to yank back his self-control.

"Your brother is angry with me."

He caught her wrists. Curled his fingers around the delicate bones and pulled her from the vehicle.

He had to touch her. Had to know that she was still there, that she hadn't vanished from his life. "You don't need to worry about him. Worry about me."

She yanked away from him.

Brodie slammed the SUV's door, and before she could flee, he pinned her against the side of the vehicle. "You aren't going to disappear."

Her dark gaze searched his. "Even if that's what is best for you?"

"Let me worry about what's best for me." His body pressed to hers. Fury was tight within him, but desire was there, too. Whenever he was close to her, need, hunger, lust built within him.

The woman was dangerous. Not to be trusted.

And he wanted her still.

"I don't want you to get hurt." Her voice was husky, seeming to stroke right over him.

"And I don't want you to get killed," Brodie told her.

Her lashes lifted.

"If you go out there alone," Brodie pushed, "with no backup, what do you think will happen?" He knew... *She'll die.*

Her hands pressed to his chest, as if she'd shove him back. She didn't, and the heat from her palms seemed to burn right through his shirt.

"I didn't think about the risk to you," Jennifer said, voice soft. "I'm so sorry. I—"

His lips took hers. The kiss was angry, because he

was angry. Angry and hungry because the woman had twisted him up with fury and desire.

Letting her go wasn't an option. Davis needed to see that. Jennifer needed to see that. He had to keep her close because if something happened to her, Brodie wasn't sure what he'd do.

When did she get to me? When did she slip beneath my guard?

She still wasn't pushing him away. Instead, Jennifer was kissing him back with a fury of her own. She'd risen onto her tiptoes and her hands now curled around his shoulders as she pressed her body to his.

She had to feel his desire. He couldn't control it and wouldn't hide it. From now on, there would be no hiding, not for either of them.

"Don't leave," he whispered against her lips.

Her head moved back a bit. Her mouth was red from his kiss. Her eyes were wide. "I never meant to hurt you or your family. When I came to the ranch before, years ago, I only wanted to repay my debt to you. I swear that was all I wanted."

He kissed her again. Pain clawed inside of him as he thought of his family, and he didn't want to head into that darkness, not then. He wanted to sink into her, to ride the rush of passion between them and to just let everything else go. He wanted to but—

He smelled smoke.

Brodie's head whipped up.

"Brodie?"

He inhaled deeply. Damn it, that *was* smoke, and the stalker who was after Jennifer had already proven just how much he liked fires.

He ran out of the garage, and his gaze immediately flew to the ranch house. Part of him had expected to see his home engulfed in flames.

It wasn't burning. *But I smell smoke.*

Davis hurried toward him. "What's happening?"

Brodie spun toward the stables. They looked fine, but he and his brother hurried inside them, checking on the horses just to be safe.

When he turned back around, Jennifer was there. Her arms were wrapped around her stomach as she stood in that open stable doorway.

He blinked, realizing she could have fled. When he'd been distracted by the scent of the smoke, Jennifer could have jumped back into his SUV and raced away.

She hadn't. She'd come to check on the horses, too.

"The fire isn't in here," Brodie said as he marched past her. He reached for her hand and pulled her with him. The night sky was dark—no stars were out, so he couldn't see anything overhead.

But the scent of smoke was drifting to him on the breeze.

"It's coming from the east," Davis muttered.

The Montgomery ranch was to the east. The

Montgomerys were the only close neighbors that the McGuires had. If you counted being ten miles away as close.

When Ava had stumbled onto the scene of their parents' murder years before, she'd saddled her horse and raced like mad toward the Montgomery ranch. Mark Montgomery had protected her, kept her safe—

We owe him.

"Let's go," Brodie said. If there was a fire out there, he had to help.

JENNIFER DIDN'T THINK they were chasing a wildfire. Not with the deadly chain of events that had become her life. So as Brodie drove his SUV toward what he'd called the Montgomery ranch and as the scent of smoke deepened in the air around them, she knew they'd be finding trouble.

Danger.

They drove through a big, open wrought-iron gate and down a long winding road that led to—

"Fire," Davis snapped. "I can see it. Damn it, his stables are burning!"

Brodie braked to a fast stop. Everyone jumped out of the vehicle and rushed toward the blaze. Jennifer could see men struggling to lead blindfolded horses out of what was quickly turning into an inferno, even as two other men tried to spray water onto the growing flames.

Davis and Brodie—they were running right toward the fire.

"Brodie!" she yelled.

He didn't stop. He ran forward. Grabbed the reins of a blindfolded horse. "I've got him, Mark," he told the man who'd been pulling the horse.

Mark immediately ran back into the flames. Davis was at his heels.

Jennifer hurried to help Brodie secure the horse, moving the animal well away from the flames. She could hear the sound of the fire crackling around her. The horses still inside the stable were screaming, terrible, desperate sounds.

She counted five horses that had been removed from the stables. How many were still inside?

Davis ran out with another horse.

The screaming continued.

While Davis brought the horse toward her, Brodie sped into the burning stables.

No!

Davis tied the horse to the tree. He coughed a bit. "I think there are four more in—"

She ran past him and into the blaze. The flames were so hot, she could feel the fire lancing over her skin. Jennifer coughed, choking on the smoke, and she crouched low as she tried to get access to clearer air. The horses were screaming, the flames still crackling—the sound eerily like laughter— and, above her, Jennifer could hear the creak and groan of wood. Was that roof about to break? To snap apart?

Fire was racing everywhere—up the walls, tearing through the hay. She fought her way to the stall on the right. A black foal was in there, huddled near the back of the stall. The foal's eyes were rolling and when she tried to approach the horse, it struck out at her.

"Easy," Jennifer whispered as she put up her hands. Could the animal even hear her over the flames? "I'm just trying to get us both out of here alive."

The foal wasn't harnessed. Jennifer grabbed for a blanket on the right, and she tried to cover the foal's eyes. The animal was shuddering and still kicking, but Jennifer managed to steer it out of the stall.

"Get out of here!" Brodie was at Jennifer's side. His face was streaked with black ash. "The roof is going to fall in!"

She pulled the foal with her. "Come on," Jennifer whispered to the foal. "Come…"

Brodie yanked the foal forward. They all tumbled outside, and Jennifer gulped in fresh air greedily. Her lungs were aching, and she couldn't seem to suck that air in fast enough—not with the coughs that racked her.

A young male—it looked as if he was in his teens—hurried forward and took the foal.

Brodie grabbed her arms. "Are you okay?"

"Y-yes..."

"What were you thinking? Why would you go in there?"

He was angry? Seriously? Because she was helping? "Why would you go in?" she yelled right back at him. "Because I didn't want to listen to those poor animals die!"

"You don't—"

"Brodie!" Davis called for his brother. "Mark is still inside. The roof is about to go, and he's in there!"

Jennifer's gaze swung toward Davis. He was running into the fire.

"No," Brodie whispered.

But Davis had gone inside.

"Brodie..."

He tore away from Jennifer and ran after his brother. Jennifer rushed forward, running behind him. Brodie had just cleared the gaping entrance to the stables when the roof collapsed.

A ball of flames seemed to fly into the dark sky.

"Brodie!" Jennifer screamed and headed right for the fire.

Hard arms grabbed her from behind. She was pulled away from the burning stables even as she fought to get inside. "Stop!" she screamed. "I need to get in there! Brodie's inside! Davis is in there and—"

"I want my brothers out, too," a rough voice growled behind her, "but I can't let you die for them."

Her head turned. She saw Mac McGuire staring back at her with wild eyes. He was as big as Brodie, just as muscled and with a grip that was just as powerful—and unbreakable.

She stopped struggling.

"Stay here," Mac ordered. "Or Brodie will kill me."

If he isn't already dead...

Then Mac freed her and shot right toward the flames. Wait, he thought she'd just stand there while he faced death? While Brodie burned? The guy didn't know her at all. But then...none of them did. No one had ever really known her.

Wasn't that the problem?

Ranch hands were still trying to spray water on the flames, but the fire was too far out of control. She knew time was of the essence. If Brodie and Davis didn't get out, they were dead.

The scene was chaos. The ranch hands were running everywhere, and two horses were racing around wildly. She dodged the horses and made her way back to—

"Got you."

Once more, hard arms had closed around Jennifer, but this time, fear raced through her. An instinctive, chilling fear. She couldn't see who held her, and when Jennifer opened up her mouth to scream, he put his hand over her mouth. She was fighting fiercely, but he was too strong for her. Every move that she used against him, every kick, every twist of her body, he seemed to anticipate.

Her captor didn't lead her toward the fire.

He didn't lead her toward the sprawling ranch house that she could see about fifty yards away.

He took her away from the light. Away from everyone else.

He's going to kill me.

Now she understood what was happening. Her stalker hadn't been able to reach her at the Mc-Guire ranch, so he'd lured her and Brodie out into the open.

Another fire...

Only she hadn't been meant to die in those flames. The fire had been the distraction. His way of catching her off guard.

She heaved against his hold, and then Jennifer felt something sharp press into her neck. A knife.

Jennifer froze, fearing that he was going to kill her right then. He could. One fast swipe of his knife, and it would be over for her.

"It won't be that easy," he whispered into her ear. "You'll suffer...just as I did." Then he kept dragging her back, far away from the others.

No, *no*! She could still see the flames. In a few more moments, she wouldn't, though, because they'd be too far away. No one would be able to help her.

Brodie. I was supposed to help Brodie! He's still in the flames!

Ignoring that knife, Jennifer drove her elbow into her attacker's gut with all her strength. Groaning, he jerked back.

She lunged forward, racing away from him as fast as she could.

Chapter Six

Brodie dragged Mark Montgomery out of the burning wreckage that had been the stables. Davis was at Brodie's side—Davis and Mac were bringing out the last stallion. Mark's prize—Legacy.

But the horse wouldn't have been worth their lives.

"Damn it, Mark, you cut it too close," Brodie snarled as he dropped his friend to the ground.

Blisters covered Mark's right arm, and his clothes were as singed as Brodie's. "Sorry…didn't mean to…risk you…"

Brodie fought to suck in a deep gulp of air. He looked down at his hands, and they were black from all the ash in the air.

Mark managed to heave himself up into a sitting position. His shoulders shook as he struggled to take in clean air, too. In the distance, Brodie could hear the wail of a fire truck's siren.

Too late.

The stables were gone.

"What the hell happened?" Brodie demanded as his gaze slid around the scene. The horses had all been corralled now. Ranch hands were still trying to put out the flames—and the flames weren't spreading, so it looked as though the ranch house was safe.

Mark coughed. "Damn thing...just seemed to explode. Heard the horses...we all raced out...fast as we could."

They'd all nearly raced to their deaths.

Brodie's gaze tracked around the scene once more. "Where is she?" He'd singed his right hand when he'd pulled Mark out from under a burning chunk of wood, but Brodie ignored the pain. He'd deal with the wound later.

"Who?" Mark muttered. Then his eyes widened. "Ava? Did you bring your sister with you?"

What? Hell, no. Ava wasn't even close by. "Jennifer," he snapped as he turned his attention to Davis. "Where is she?"

But Davis wouldn't know. Davis had been in that burning building when Brodie left Jennifer. Brodie had run back in *because* he sure as hell hadn't planned to leave his fool brother and Mark there to burn.

"She tried to go in...after you," Mac said, coughing into his fist. "I'd just gotten here. Heard the call on the police scanner when I was heading for our ranch." He ran a weary hand over the back of his neck. "I stopped her from going into the fire. Told her to stay back or you'd have my head."

He searched the area once more. There was no sign of her.

He whirled back around, stared at the fire. *Don't be inside...* Terror started to rip through him.

"She ran away," Davis muttered, voice tired, angry. "Should have seen it coming...took the first opportunity and ran. That was her plan, right?"

Mark staggered to his feet. "Who are we talking about?"

Brodie knew he was going back into the flames. If Jennifer was in there—

"Help!"

He whipped around even as the scream died away. His gaze flew to the left. To the right.

"Brodie." Davis frowned at him. "Man, look, you knew she wanted to run, so—"

"Didn't you just hear her scream?" A woman who'd run away on her own wouldn't scream.

And she wouldn't leave me to the fire.

Davis hesitated, then shook his head.

Brodie glared at Mac. "You heard her, right?" His heart was thundering in his chest.

"No, I just hear those damn flames."

He'd *heard* her cry. Brodie knew that he had. So he took off, running toward the trees—trees that would eventually separate the Montgomery property from the McGuire ranch.

I'm coming, Jennifer. I'm coming!

His feet pounded against the earth as he ran as fast as he could because he knew with utter certainty Jennifer had just screamed.

Help.

HE'D CAUGHT HER. He'd tackled her, and Jennifer had screamed as loudly as she could right before her body had slammed into the dirt. He held her there, pinned beneath him, and the knife was back at her throat.

But he said he wasn't going to kill me quickly. His mistake. He'd given her an advantage by letting her know that death wasn't imminent.

"The SEAL can't save you this time," he told her.

Maybe. Maybe she could save herself just fine.

His voice was so low and rasping. Was he trying to disguise it? Or just make sure that no one overheard him?

His hand fisted in her hair. "I don't need you awake for this part."

She knew he was about to knock her out. She clenched her teeth against the pain as she tried to twist her body away from his. She needed to see his face. "Get away from me!"

She rolled and twisted. The knife cut over her shoulder, and she was pretty sure she lost way too much hair, but she managed to get a few feet away from him. She crawled back, spiderlike.

"No one can hear your screams." He stood. It was so dark—he was just a menacing shadow as he closed in once more. "Not over the crackle of those flames. Not over the cries from the horses. You could scream until you had no breath, and no one but me would hear you."

She was hearing him loud and clear, and, now that he'd stopped using that thick whisper, his voice seemed familiar to her. "I...know you."

He laughed then. "Almost intimately."

Ice squeezed her heart.

"Was it all a game?" he suddenly asked her. "How many others did you lure in? Only to turn on them, just as you did me?"

Clinging tightly to a tree, she pulled herself up to her feet. She still couldn't place his voice. *But I know him.*

"I went to hell because of you, dear Jennifer. A living hell. And before I'm done with you, I promise that you'll share my nightmare."

She already was. *I need a weapon.*

"Now, we're leaving here. You can fight me if you want. That will just give me a reason to hurt you more..." He laughed again, and the chill around her grew worse. "As if I need a reason."

She wasn't leaving with him. She was dead if she left. And she was dead if she didn't get away from him right then.

"Jennifer!" That roar was her name, and she could hear it so clearly—because it was close.

Brodie! He'd gotten out of the flames. He'd heard her cries. "I'm here!" she called out, lunging away from the tree. "I'm—"

Her attacker caught her and slammed her head into the tree. The hit was hard, brutal, and Jennifer's body slumped forward as everything went completely black around her.

"I'M HERE!"

Brodie jerked at Jennifer's desperate cry.

"I'm—"

Her scream was cut off.

He was already racing straight ahead. Racing and—

He burst through the trees. Brodie saw a man in black, a man who had Jennifer slung over his shoulder.

"Put her down!" Brodie shouted.

The man stilled. He didn't look back at Brodie. "This isn't your fight."

Brodie bent and yanked a knife from his ankle holster. He always kept that knife close. Jennifer wasn't moving. She hung limply over the man's shoulder. *What did that guy do to her?* "It damn well is my fight." *Because Jennifer is mine.* "Now put her down and back away!"

The man backed away, sliding deeper into the

covering of the trees, but he didn't free Jennifer. "Why does it matter to you? Why does she matter?"

"Let. Her. Go."

"She's a liar. She'll betray you the same way she did me."

Brodie's fingers tightened around the knife.

"The SEAL," the man murmured. "You think you're the hero? Hasn't she already brought enough torment to your life?"

A low moan came from Jennifer.

"Walk away," the man said in a rasping voice. "And I won't destroy your family."

Brodie took a step forward. "Let her go." *I will destroy you, no matter what.*

The fellow slid Jennifer off his shoulder, but he didn't free her. Her body swayed in front of him as he held her with a steely grip. "In case you can't see it," the jerk told him, voice chillingly calm, "I have a knife at her throat. One fast move and she's gone."

"In case you can't see it," Brodie snapped right back, "I have a knife in my hand, and my brother Davis has a gun pointed at the back of your head."

Silence. *Didn't see that coming, did you?* "Now let her go!" Brodie ordered.

The man threw Jennifer forward. Her body pitched toward the ground, and Brodie lunged to grab her. He caught Jennifer right before she would have slammed, face-first, into the earth.

Footsteps thundered as the man ran away. Brodie wanted to rush after him—he'd been bluffing about Davis and his gun—but when he touched Jennifer's hair, he felt something sticky and wet.

Blood.

"Jennifer?"

Her head sagged back against his arm.

"Jennifer!" His hand found the hard, bleeding knot on her head, and when his fingers slid down to her shoulder, he could feel her blood there, too. "It's all right, sweetheart," he promised as he lifted her carefully into his arms. "I've got you."

He had to get her out of there. The attacker had vanished, but at any moment, the man could strike again—with his knife or any other weapon that the guy had on him.

Brodie backed away, his heart racing too fast in his chest. Jennifer was a deadweight in his arms, and fear was growing within him. Head wounds could be so tricky, so deadly. "Hold on," he whispered to her.

Then he heard the sound of rushing footsteps coming from the right. The Montgomery ranch was to the right and—

He heard a high-pitched whistle. An old signal that he and Davis had used since they were kids. Brodie whistled back, and, seconds later, Davis was in his path.

"What happened to her?" Davis asked. He came closer, and Brodie saw the gun in his hands.

If only Davis had been there a few minutes sooner.

"Her stalker is here... He hurt her." He jerked his head to indicate direction. "The guy ran that way—he's armed."

"On it." Davis brushed by him. Stopped. "You got her?"

His hold tightened on Jennifer. Normally, he'd be joining Davis on this hunt, but not when Jennifer was hurt. Not when she needed him. "I've got her." And he wasn't letting go.

Davis headed into the darkness. He could handle himself, Brodie knew it, but...

"Be careful," he growled after his brother because he could still hear the stalker's threat. *I'll destroy your family.*

The hell he would.

THE MOTORCYCLE WAS just where he'd left it. He jumped on the bike and sped away from the Montgomery ranch as if the damn devil were chasing him. *Maybe he is.*

He kept his lights off as he headed down the dirt road. He wasn't looking to attract any more attention. Not then.

Brodie McGuire had Jennifer.

She'd been his for the taking. Justice had been at

hand, but Brodie had interfered. Again. He'd tried to warn the man. After all, his battle wasn't with the McGuires.

He'd done his research on that family once he'd learned of Jennifer's connection to them. All the McGuire brothers were supposed to be tough and deadly, all ex-military. They played hard, and they didn't mind getting their hands dirty—or bloody.

He hadn't wanted them as enemies. He'd just wanted his pound of flesh from Jennifer.

He'd told Brodie to walk way. He'd warned the man.

Why wouldn't he listen? Why was Brodie so connected to Jennifer?

She must have pulled him into her web, too. Jennifer, so tempting, so beguiling with her wide, dark eyes and that slow smile. Once she'd made him think that she was actually falling for him.

Until the authorities had come for him.

Until he'd woken in that cell.

So many days of torment. One after the other.

He wasn't going to let her get away. Jennifer wouldn't escape his punishment, and if Brodie McGuire wouldn't get out of his way, then he would have to take out the ex-SEAL.

I warned you, McGuire. You should have listened.

There would be no more warnings.

SHE WAS IN an ambulance, and the shriek of the siren was making her head hurt. Jennifer groaned as the EMT leaned over her.

"Ma'am, are you in pain?" He touched her forehead, and her breath hissed out. "You've got a concussion. We're taking you to the hospital."

She grabbed his hand. "Where's Brodie? Brodie McGuire?"

He didn't answer her quickly enough, and she shot upright. Nausea rolled through her as the pounding in her head grew about a hundred times worse. "Did he get out of the stables? Is he—"

"I'm right here."

Her head turned. Brodie was standing just beyond the open ambulance doors. Jennifer's breath came out in a relieved rush. "I was afraid you were trapped in there. In the fire."

His gaze searched hers. "Do you remember what happened?"

She remembered the flames. Her fear. Her—

"Ma'am, you need to let me finish my exam." Jennifer realized she had a death grip on the EMT's hand.

"He was here." Her stalker. He'd been at the scene. He'd hurt her. Her breath came faster, and her heartbeat doubled.

"Ma'am, you need to calm down."

Her gaze was still on Brodie. "Did you see him?" He must have… The last thing she remembered was

Brodie calling her name. He'd been in the woods. Brodie must have found her and stopped the guy who'd been attacking her. "Do the cops have him?" she asked before he could respond. "Where is he?" She needed to see his face. To stare into the eyes of the man who'd tried to destroy her. *I need to find out why.*

Brodie's face tensed. "He got away."

Her racing heartbeat stopped.

Brodie jumped into the ambulance.

The EMT tried to push him back out, but Brodie ignored the tech. "Davis is searching for him. Mac is combing the woods. We're going to get him."

She let go of the EMT. Her hand rose to her shoulder. Jennifer remembered the slash of the knife against her skin. She flinched when she felt the bandage that had been placed there. "He…he started the fire in the stables." *He could have killed you!* "Your friend, is he—"

"Everyone got out."

"Uh, excuse me." The EMT's face had reddened. "I need to take care of her. You two can talk at the hospital."

She didn't want to leave Brodie. There were so many questions she needed to ask him, but the pounding in her head was growing worse and spots were starting to appear around her eyes.

Jennifer slid back down onto the stretcher. "I'm glad you're safe. That everyone's…safe." Because if anyone had been hurt, it would have been on her. She'd brought this danger right to all of them.

"Sir, you have to leave now," the EMT said.

Brodie leaned toward Jennifer. "I'll be following right behind the ambulance."

Tears stung her eyes. Jennifer managed a small nod. "I'm sorry."

A muscle flexed in his jaw. "If I'd gotten there a few minutes later, he would have already taken you away from me." The words were a dark rumble. "What would I have done then?"

Before she could think of any kind of answer, Brodie slid out of the ambulance. The EMT leaned over her and started asking her how many fingers she saw.

She pushed his hand out of her way. Jennifer craned her neck so that she could stare at Brodie. "What would I have done without you?" she whispered.

Another EMT slammed the ambulance doors, blocking her view of him. A few moments later, the ambulance lurched away.

BRODIE PACED THE hospital waiting room. Just being in that place made him too damn tense. He'd been in this hospital a few months back, when his brother Grant had been injured—and that scene sure hadn't ended well.

He went up to the nurse's desk for the fourth time. "Can I see her yet?"

The nurse, an older woman with stern blue eyes, frowned at him. "Sir, I've told you that your fiancée is still being examined—"

The wide doors swung open behind her. A doctor appeared—the doctor who'd been checking out Jennifer. When he saw Brodie, the man nodded.

Brodie gave up his post near the nurse. "I want to see her," he told the doctor flatly.

The doc nodded. "Right...and she wants to see you, too." He cleared his throat. "She is also rather adamantly insisting that she be released. I can't keep her here, but I think the woman needs—"

The door opened again. Jennifer was there, wearing a hospital gown, a bandage on her forehead and a very determined-looking expression on her face.

Brodie pretty much jumped toward her. "What are you doing?" And he pulled her against him, holding her carefully. "You aren't supposed to be walking around out here!"

"They took my clothes, so I had to come out like this." She sounded disgruntled. "Why'd they take my clothes?"

The doctor cleared his throat. "Uh, miss, your clothes were taken because they were covered in blood and ash. We bagged them for you—"

Jennifer turned in Brodie's arms. "Please take me out of here," she whispered to him. "He could come for me here. I'm not safe." Her voice didn't carry past him.

He tensed against her. Davis had been attacked in the same hospital. The attack had come when Davis was trying to protect Grant's fiancée…only Scarlett hadn't been his fiancée back then. Scarlett had been lured away from Grant's bedside. Davis had tried to guard her, but he'd been shot.

He was bleeding out in front of me.

That hospital held far too many bad memories for Brodie. And Jennifer was right—the security at that place left a whole hell of a lot to be desired.

But with her concussion…

He glanced at the doctor. The man sighed. "She can leave. But keep her monitored, you understand? If she sleeps, wake her up every two hours to assess her condition. If you see her exhibiting any signs of confusion or if her nausea gets worse, contact the hospital immediately." He frowned at Jennifer. "I would feel better if you stayed for observation but—"

"There's no way I'm staying," she said. Her hold tightened on Brodie. "Please, just get me out of here."

His gaze held the doctor's for a moment longer.

"When you check on her, ask her name," the doctor added. "Review her vitals. Even if she's progressing well, I want her brought back in within twenty-four hours so that I can assess her once more."

"Anything else?" Brodie asked.

"Take care of her," the doctor said, then nodded, giving the all clear.

"Always," Brodie promised. Then he bent his head toward Jennifer. "On our way, sweetheart," Brodie whispered as he lifted her into his arms. He held her carefully, cradling her as he walked past the nurses' station.

"You take good care of your fiancée!" the nurse called after him.

Jennifer stirred a bit in Brodie's arms. They slipped into the elevator, and when those doors closed, Jennifer peeked up at him from beneath her long lashes. "I've got a bump on my head and a scratch on my shoulder. I can walk."

"And I can carry you." He liked holding her. "So let me."

Her breath sighed out and blew lightly against his throat. "I'm your fiancée?" she asked softly. "I don't remember you proposing."

Despite everything that was happening, his lips almost twitched. "Probably your concussion," he told her. "I've heard those can make folks forget things."

She laughed then. A sweet, light sound that made his chest feel funny. He pulled her even closer against him. When the elevator doors opened into the parking garage, he carried her back to his SUV.

He put her down long enough to do a sweep of

the vehicle—the last thing he wanted was another explosion; then he settled her inside, adjusting her gown, and he realized… *She doesn't have shoes on!*

His laughter came then, unexpected. Rough. Relieved…*She's alive. She's safe…with me.*

He shut her door and hurried around to the driver's side of the vehicle. His door slammed behind him, and Brodie reached out to start the SUV, but Jennifer's hand closed around his.

"He got away, didn't he?"

His head turned toward her. The laughter had faded completely as the fear came back. He wasn't used to fear, and the emotion made him angry. "For now."

She gave a little nod. "He'll be back. He won't stop."

No, Brodie didn't think he would stop. Not until the guy had gotten what he wanted.

And what he wanted…that was Jennifer.

"Don't take me back to the ranch," she whispered. "He'll strike there next. He could go after your stables or your house and—"

"The security we have is too good. That's why he hit the Montgomery ranch. He wanted to draw you out. To make you vulnerable." He cranked the SUV and drove them away from the hospital. "Our ranch is the best place for you."

"Not if I'm putting a target on your home."

The stalker's words played through Brodie's

mind. *I'll destroy your family.* "This whole thing is personal," Brodie said. "He knows you."

"Almost intimately," she whispered.

His gaze shot to her. "What?" Now the fear was totally overpowered by the fury pumping through him.

She rubbed her eyes. "That's what he told me… That we almost knew each other intimately."

"I asked you about former lovers—"

"He wasn't my lover." Her voice was adamant. "But…I knew his voice… It was so familiar." Her hand fell to her lap. "I just have to remember him. I have to remember *who* he is. Then I can understand why he hates me so much. Why he wants to hurt me."

But he didn't want to just hurt Jennifer. Brodie knew the man out there wanted to kill her.

And I won't let that happen.

THE MCGUIRE RANCH rose before her. The gates were imposing. The house a strong, solid structure against the night.

Brodie opened her door. Offered her his hand. She started to slide down to the ground, but he caught her and lifted Jennifer up against him.

"I think we covered this," she whispered as her hands curled around his neck. "I really am quite good at walking." And she'd had much worse injuries over the years. The slice on her shoulder hadn't even required stitches.

Ignoring her words, Brodie carried her into the house. He checked the security system. Then, still holding her, he took her down the hallway.

He didn't go to the guest room.

Brodie carried her inside *his* room.

"Brodie?"

"The doctor said I should wake you every two hours." He lowered her onto the bed. "This way, I can keep you close. It will be easier for me to check you here."

She sat up quickly. The paper gown rasped over her skin. "I can stay in the other room. I don't even have to sleep."

He stared down at her. "You're afraid to stay with me."

She shook her head.

He turned away. Reached into a drawer and pulled out a T-shirt. "You want to change into this? You'll be more comfortable." His voice was carefully emotionless as he brought the shirt toward her.

She reached for the shirt.

His gaze slid over her. She felt that caress like a touch. *I want his touch.* She always did.

Her fingers curled into the fabric. "You're going to…to turn away while I change, right?"

His lips quirked. Those sexy dimples of his almost flashed. "Why would I do that?" One dark brow lifted.

She felt heat stain her cheeks. She should really be past the blushing stage, but with him, she wasn't. "Brodie…"

Sighing, he turned away from her, giving her the broad expanse of his back.

Jennifer fumbled and got rid of that horrible paper gown, and she slid on his soft T-shirt. She'd worn his shirt before, and, well, she liked wearing his clothes. Like the previous shirt, this one smelled of him. That rich, masculine scent. She tugged down the hem of the shirt. It came all the way to her thighs and—

"Can I turn around now?"

"Yes." Why was her voice so shaky? She'd faced off against killers. She'd sent countless criminals to jail. She shouldn't be nervously stuttering just because she was in Brodie McGuire's bed.

But she was.

Get a grip, woman.

He yanked off the shirt he'd been wearing and tossed it aside. His shoes followed. As he turned toward her, Brodie's hands went to his belt.

So did her gaze.

"Don't worry, I won't ask *you* to turn away," he murmured.

Her eyes snapped right back to his face. "What are you doing?"

Those dimples of his definitely flashed then. "Getting undressed so that I can get into bed with you."

"I think that's a bad idea." But her words sounded husky and inviting—definitely not her plan—and her tone sure implied she thought he'd just told her the best idea ever.

His hands stilled. "I'm not going to make love to you."

Now she was fisting her hands around the sheets. Is that how he thought of it? As making love with her? She hadn't realized—

"Not while you're hurt." He kicked his jeans aside to reveal a sexy pair of boxers that rode low on his hips. "But as soon as you're better, sweetheart, you will be mine again."

Her gaze was back to raking over him. He had the best physique that she'd ever seen. So strong and muscled. Powerful.

He was also climbing into bed with her. Jennifer shook her head. "Davis will come home soon." She figured the guy had to turn up sooner or later. "If I'm in here with you in the morning, he'll think we were...together."

Brodie laughed at that. "We have been together."

That wasn't what she'd meant.

"And, besides," Brodie added as the back of his hand slid down her cheek in a brief caress, "I don't really care what Davis thinks about the two of us. As long as he knows that he needs to keep his hands off you, I'm fine."

He leaned over her. Jennifer stopped breathing as she stared into his eyes.

"Relax," Brodie whispered. "I'm just turning off the light." His fingers flicked the switch on the lamp. The room plunged into darkness.

Then he slid back to his side of the bed. Jennifer gingerly lowered herself down fully on the mattress. Despite her exhaustion, adrenaline still pumped through her. Sleep wasn't going to come easily, so Brodie didn't exactly have to worry about that whole waking-every-two-hours routine that the doctor had prescribed.

Her head brushed against the pillow. In the dark, she found it was easier to talk with him. "You saved me again."

The sheets rustled. Had he turned to stare at her? He wouldn't be able to see much of her in that sheltering darkness.

"He wanted to take me away to torture me." Fear was there now, and it wouldn't go away, not until they caught her stalker. "He doesn't plan to make my death easy."

His arm curled around her stomach. He *had* turned toward her in the dark. His touch made her feel safer.

"I don't care what he has planned," Brodie muttered. "He's not hurting you again."

If Brodie hadn't heard her screams, the stalker would be hurting her right then. Instead, she was safe in Brodie's arms. He pulled her closer, and she rested her head on his shoulder. It felt…strangely right to be there with him.

"Tell me who you were…" His voice seemed to rumble all around her. "Before you became Jennifer Wesley."

"I was lost." That was the way she'd always thought of herself. "My parents died when I was just a kid. A drunk driver hit them." And they'd just been…gone. "I was ten, angry with the world and hurting all the time." The social workers had said she was acting out each time she got in trouble. They'd told her that if she wanted a real family, she had to show how good she could be.

But she'd already had a real family. A family that had been stolen from her.

"I bounced around the foster system for a while. Back then, I had a rule about getting close to people."

"A rule?"

"Yes. The rule was…*never get close.*" That was the same rule she'd lived by when she worked for the government. And that rule had slowly become a way of life for her.

Never get close. Because when people got too close, you became vulnerable. You needed them, and you…you hurt when they left.

There were only two people who'd ever made Jennifer break her rule. Slowly, over time, she'd softened toward Nate. Maybe she'd even started to see him as the father she'd lost.

And…

She'd let Brodie get close. So very close.

"Who were you back then? Tell me your name."

Her breath slid out on a soft sigh. "Jennifer Belmont. Jenny." Little Jenny Belmont from Florence, Idaho. "No one really knew me there." Sometimes, she'd felt invisible in that town. "So when I vanished and became someone else… Well, there wasn't exactly anyone around to care." That was precisely why the US government had recruited her for the job.

Too late, she'd learned that she was one of the expendable ones. If she'd died on one of the missions, if she'd been killed on foreign land, then there would have been no outcry from desperate family members and friends. There would have been…nothing.

And that was why Brodie's rescue had surprised her so much. She'd given up hope by the time he came for her.

Then he'd brought that hope right back to her.

"What did Jenny Belmont like to do?"

Had she just felt him press a kiss to her temple? She wasn't sure. "She…liked to read, a lot." Because that had been her escape. "She rode horses when she could. When she saved up enough money to go for a ride at the local stables." She'd felt so free when she raced on those horses. "Her mother had loved horses, so she liked them, too. It made her feel close to—"

"You."

"What?"

"You keep referring to your younger self as 'she' as if Jenny is a separate person from you."

Didn't he realize? She was. Jenny Belmont was a lifetime away from Jennifer Wesley.

"*You* liked to read. *You* loved to ride horses. That's still you, deep inside. Jenny Belmont didn't die, no matter what those government suits might have wanted you to believe." His fingers slid down, pressed over her heart. Her heart was galloping like mad beneath his touch. "Inside, it's just…*you*."

She was glad they were in the dark. Jennifer didn't want him seeing her tears. "What about you?" Jennifer whispered. "Will you tell me what Brodie McGuire was like…before he became a SEAL?" His hand was still over her heart, but he adjusted their bodies, cradling her against him.

"I was a hell-raiser."

What?

"Always getting into trouble. Always messing

with Davis. I've given him hell all my life, but he's always there for me. So are all my brothers. So is Ava."

She pressed closer to him. "I kind of pictured you as the quarterback…maybe homecoming king…"

He laughed. She realized she loved the rough sound of his laughter.

"Sweetheart," he murmured, "I was too busy racing my horse and raising hell for that. I lived for danger back then—"

"You still do," she pointed out. "It's not like SEALs live the safe and easy life."

"No." His hand stroked over her hair. "But I became a SEAL to make a difference. I grew up and wanted to do more."

Like save a stranger from death.

"I'm sorry about your parents," she told him. "So sorry." She'd liked his mother. Brodie had her smile. The woman had been so kind but…

There was fear in her eyes when we met.

Jennifer didn't tell Brodie that. Not then. He kept stroking her hair.

Her eyes drifted closed.

"I dreamed about you…"

She was almost asleep when she heard his soft words.

"And I wished so many damn times that I hadn't just let you walk away from me…"

She felt the press of his lips against her temple once more.

"I won't make that mistake again."

Chapter Seven

"Jennifer, wake up." The voice was deep and rumbling, sexy and dark.

Her eyelids slowly lifted.

"Do you know who I am?"

She stared into the most gorgeous green eyes she'd ever seen. "I dreamed about you, too…"

He frowned at her. "Who am I?"

"Brodie." Her lips curled. She lifted her arms, looping them around his neck. "In my dreams, you didn't let me walk away."

Right then, it was hard to separate her dreams from reality.

"Kiss me?" Jennifer whispered.

"Sweetheart, I'm supposed to be checking—"

She pulled him toward her. He pressed his lips to hers.

Not a dream.

Her mouth opened beneath his, and his tongue slid past her lips. She pressed closer to him, wanting more, as her body seemed to ignite from the kiss.

One kiss shouldn't make her body quiver. It shouldn't make need, desire, grow—hot and dark and fast—within her. But it did. Because that was what *he* did to her.

"Jennifer." Her name was a growl of desire. "Not yet…The doctor said I had to take care of you."

She knew how he could take care of her. How she could take care of him.

He kissed her again. "Not yet…"

She stared into his gaze. Sunlight trickled through the blinds, and she could easily see the desire on his face.

"But soon," Brodie added, voice a bit ragged, "I'll take what we both want."

"Promises, promises," Jennifer whispered before she drifted to sleep once more.

BRODIE WATCHED HER SLEEP. He'd been checking on her every two hours.

He brushed back her hair. She murmured something in her sleep. Brodie leaned closer to her. "What? Jennifer, what did you—"

"Stay with me."

His chest ached at those words. "I am. I will." He wasn't about to let her face the danger alone.

He'd never forget the terror he'd felt when he raced through the woods. Davis had been so confident that she'd snuck away on her own, but he'd known, he'd *known*, that she hadn't left him. Not to the fire.

And he'd been so afraid that he wouldn't be able to find her.

You won't take her from me. He didn't know who that sicko was out there, but the man had made a deadly mistake.

Brodie wasn't going to let the guy attack his friends or his family. No matter what he had to do, Brodie would take the man down.

His gaze slid over Jennifer's face. *I'll stop him, and then you'll be safe...*

She'd come back to him, and Brodie had no intention of letting her go again.

"JENNIFER." HE SAID her name softly because he didn't want to scare her. The back of his hand slid down the silk of her arm. "I need you to wake up for me."

Her lashes fluttered as her head turned toward him. "Was...dreaming about you again." Her eyes met his. He got lost in the darkness of her stare.

"What's my name?" he asked her because that was supposed to be part of the drill the doctor had given him.

She smiled at him then, even as she stretched, catlike and sexy, in his bed. "Brodie."

His name was a husky whisper on her lips.

"You're Brodie, and I'm Jennifer." A slight pause,

then, "And I'm not delusional. I'm not seeing double. I'm totally fine."

Had he ever told her that she was the sexiest woman he'd ever seen?

"Brodie?" Her smile slipped. "What's wrong?"

"You never would have come back…if you hadn't been in danger."

Her lashes flickered. "What do you mean?"

"I wouldn't have seen you again." He had to kiss her. He leaned forward. Pressed a kiss to her full lips. "And that would have been a damn shame."

A rap sounded at his door. "Brodie?" Davis called. "We need to talk."

Davis had the worst timing in the world. The absolute worst. One day, he'd have to find a way of paying the guy back for all that crappy timing.

"I put fresh clothes in the bathroom for you," he said as he stared down at Jennifer "Get dressed and come out whenever you're ready." Before he could move away, her hand swept out and her fingers circled around his wrist.

"Brodie?" Davis called again.

"I'm coming." He'd locked the door, so Davis wasn't about to just barge in—even though his brother had a habit of butting in where he didn't always belong.

Brodie glanced down at Jennifer's hand. Her fingers looked so delicate around his bigger, darker wrist.

"Thank you," she told him. "For the clothes, for saving my life—for everything."

He shook his head. "I don't want gratitude from you."

"Then what do you want?"

He stared down at her.

When he heard her quick inhale, Brodie knew that she'd seen the desire in his eyes. Good. He'd wanted her to know exactly how he felt and to know what he needed from her. "Everything." As he'd held her in his arms as she slept, Brodie had realized he wouldn't settle for anything less.

Her fingers slipped away from him.

"And that's what I'll take," he promised her, then he left her there, in his bed.

BRODIE AND DAVIS walked toward the bluff. It was a beautiful spot, an oasis right in the middle of nowhere... Or at least, that's what Brodie's father had said about the place. The family had originally bought the land so long ago because of the lake— because of the bluff. Because of the beauty they could see there and the hope for their futures.

Their great-grandparents had been immigrants from Ireland. Desperate, looking for a fresh start, they'd come to the United States.

They'd found a new home. A new life. The land there had belonged to his family for over a hundred years.

The memories are good and bad here. His father's words drifted through his mind. Words that his father had said months before his death. *This place shapes us. It's not just dirt and water. It's our lives. Our home.*

Brodie hadn't been able to let go of that home.

"You're treading into some dangerous water with her," Davis said as he looked out at the lake.

"I'm not afraid of rough water." Since when did a SEAL fear that?

"Maybe you should be afraid. The fire in those stables…That was a damn near thing. Mark could have died. *You* could have died—"

"He didn't. None of us did." While Davis was staring at the lake, Brodie was staring at his brother's profile. "He almost took her away from me."

Davis glanced at him.

"If I hadn't heard her scream…" He shook his head. Davis had been so sure that she'd run off on her own, but Brodie's gut had told him otherwise. "I don't know what I would have done."

Davis stepped toward him. "You're not saying—"

"I never forgot her. I couldn't. Six years… Hell, I should have put her in my past. But she kept staying in my head. I'd catch myself wondering what she was doing. Who she was with." He'd hated the flashes of jealousy. "Then she walked right through my door. She came back to me."

A frustrated snarl slipped from his brother. "She's tied up with our parents' death!"

"She didn't kill them—you know that."

"She could have led the killers right to them! She—"

"Jennifer is a victim."

Davis shook his head. "By her own admission, the woman is a trained agent. Her livelihood was lies. *Lies.* How can you believe anything she says? Anything she does?"

He just stared back at Davis. When it came to Jennifer, Brodie wouldn't back down, not even for his twin.

"This isn't like you." Davis regarded him with a puzzled expression. "You don't get involved with women this way. You hook up. You move on. You—"

"You ever wonder why I moved on so much?"

"What?" Davis appeared lost.

"They weren't her."

Davis squeezed his eyes shut. "No. Do not tell me this stuff. Do not."

"I'm not moving on this time."

"Hell." The word was both dismayed and resigned.

But Brodie wasn't done yet. "Whatever happens, whatever we find out…I want you to back me up. I want you…I want you to protect her." *In case something happens and I can't…*

Davis turned away and went back to staring at that water. "Don't I always back you up? Hell, I joined the Navy, I became a SEAL, just because you needed someone to watch your back."

Surprise pushed through Brodie. "But...but I thought you—"

"You're my kid brother," Davis muttered. "What else was I supposed to do?"

Davis was older by all of five minutes.

"Protecting my family—that's all I've ever wanted to do. But it's the one thing I just can't seem to get right."

Brodie strode forward. He caught Davis's shoulder and swung him around so that they faced off.

"I don't trust her," Davis said flatly. "She's not the innocent you think. She's not—"

"The first time I saw her, Jennifer was tied to a chair in a dirty, dark room. Her wrists were bleeding. Her face was bruised. The men who had her... they had left for just a few moments, and I knew that I didn't have long to get her out of there."

A furrow appeared between Davis's brows. "Why are you telling me this?"

"I made my way to her. She whispered one thing to me. Just one thing."

Davis waited.

"She told me to leave because there wasn't time to free her. To go because she didn't want anyone dying for her." He shook his head. "Bleeding and beaten, and she was still trying to protect me."

Maybe that was when it had happened. When the ice around his heart had cracked and she'd first slipped inside.

"The alarm sounded before I got her clear of that place. My men had to engage the enemy, and I had to run like hell with her." He could still hear the thunder of gunfire. The screams. But none of those screams had come from Jennifer. "She didn't make a sound, not the whole time we were escaping. She didn't have on shoes, her clothes were torn…and she ran for miles with me without saying a single word." His mouth hitched as he remembered. "And when the enemy almost got a shot at me, she was the one to shove me out of the way. I was there to save her, but she…she saved me."

Davis rocked back on his heels. "She had your back."

Yes, she had. "Now I've got hers," he said simply.

Davis looked away.

"I made love with her when we were safe. I… Damn, I knew better. Knew that one move could have cost me my career and a hell of a lot more, but nothing could have kept me from her then." He waited for Davis to glance back at him. When he did, Brodie finished, "And nothing will keep me from her now."

Nothing…no one.

After a moment, Davis nodded. "I understand."
Davis always had understood him.

"Whatever happens," Davis told him quietly,
"she'll be protected."

Good. That was what he'd needed to hear—

"Brodie?"

He glanced over at the soft call and saw Jennifer walking toward them, her steps slow, uncertain. She'd dressed in a pair of his sister's jeans,
a loose shirt and a pair of brown boots. Jennifer
had removed the bandage near her forehead, and he
could see the bruising from her attack. She hesitated
as her gaze darted between him and Davis. "Is…
everything all right?"

He nodded. Brodie thought everything was perfectly clear to Davis now. "I want to head over to
the Montgomery ranch and see if anyone saw anything before the fire."

"I want to come," she said quickly.

Like he would have left her behind. That wasn't
an option for him any longer. The memory of her
scream would haunt him forever. Until they caught
that fire-happy SOB, Brodie intended to stay as
close to her as possible. "Then let's go." He walked
forward. Took her arm.

"Jennifer."

She glanced over at Davis's call. So did Brodie.
"Watch his back," Davis told her.

She inclined her head toward him. Her hair slid over her shoulders. "Always."

JENNIFER DIDN'T KNOW who he was. After all she'd done to wreck his life, the woman had truly forgotten him. Walked away, never glanced back and gone on to destroy other lives.

He could barely contain his fury. He'd been right in front of her, touching her, hurting her.

And she still hadn't known who he was.

Sure, he'd changed in the years. He wasn't the polished millionaire any longer. He didn't wear three-piece suits and go to the gym four times a week. He didn't drive fancy cars or dine at the best restaurants.

He hunted. He killed.

She'd taken that other world away, turning him into someone who lived in the shadows. Someone who'd fought for his very food, his survival. Someone who'd lost everything…someone with nothing to lose.

Before she died, Jennifer would scream his name. She would know exactly who she faced in those final moments. She'd beg forgiveness. He would make certain of it.

I will not be forgotten.

Perhaps it was time to involve the other player in this game a bit more. The man had been in the background so far, slowly setting up Jennifer… But, yes, now it was time for him to earn his money.

Time for him to deliver Jennifer on a silver platter.

Put a knife in her back, and let her see how that betrayal feels…

He lifted up the phone and called the man who'd been hiding in Austin, the man who'd first led him to Jennifer.

THE REMAINS OF the Montgomery stables were a charred black mess. Jennifer slammed the door of the SUV and stared at the solemn sight, her body trembling.

She'd taken off the bandage on her head. The bump had gone down, and now there was just bruising along her hairline. She still had the bandage on her shoulder, and every time she thought of that knife…

I can't let him get close to me again.

His voice replayed through her mind again and again, so familiar but—

I can't place him.

If only it had been lighter, if the stars had been shining, if the moon had been out and she'd been able to see her attacker.

"At least the horses are safe." A man with tousled blond hair and tired eyes walked toward them.

"Mark." Brodie met him, slapped the guy on the shoulder. "So damn sorry this happened."

Mark glanced at the stables. "We'll rebuild."

Jennifer edged closer to the men.

"The fire spread so fast. The flames were racing into the sky before I knew what was happening." Mark's shoulders rolled back as he exhaled on a long sigh. "And Davis…he was still here when the fire marshal came out. Your brother told the guy it was arson." His brows rose. "Arson? When he first said that, I couldn't understand why somebody would want to torch my stables."

Because the man who did this was trying to get to me.

Brodie glanced at Jennifer; then he told Mark, "We think the fire was a trap. The man who set it…he wanted to lure Jennifer and me over here. He wanted us vulnerable."

"Jennifer." Mark said her name as if tasting it. Then he looked toward her, shaking his head. "Sorry, ma'am, we didn't meet before, did we? Not in the middle of that nightmare." He gave her a firm nod. "I'm Mark. Mark Montgomery." He offered his hand.

Her fingers wrapped around his. It felt so wrong to be shaking his hand as if they were friends or going to be friends. He'd just lost his stables because of her. "He's hunting me," Jennifer said as she held on to his hand. "And you were hurt because of that."

Mark glanced at Brodie, but he didn't free her hand. Anger hardened his jaw. "All right... So then I guess my first question is what can I do to help find this jerk?"

Surprise rippled through her.

"This isn't your fight," Brodie said as he pulled Jennifer away from Mark and back to his side. "I'll find the guy. I'll stop him."

But Mark shook his head. He was close to Brodie's height, with shoulders that were nearly as wide and an expression just as fierce as Brodie's. "He made it my fight." His voice had a harsh intensity. "My men could have died. *I* could have died. You think I'm just going to turn the other cheek after that? You know that's not who I am."

"My brothers and I are after him..."

Mark focused on Jennifer once more. "Why did he want to draw you out?"

"Because he wants to hurt me." She forced herself to speak without emotion. "Torture me slowly, then eventually kill me."

Mark swore.

"And that's not happening," Brodie snarled.

She rather hoped it didn't. "I didn't mean to bring my storm to your door," Jennifer told Mark.

"Lots of storms have been at my door." His reply was soft. "And I'm still standing."

"If you want to help us," Brodie said, "then tell us what you saw before the fire. Let us talk to your ranch hands. We need to know if they caught sight of the man who did this."

"You can talk to them all, but it won't do you any good. I've questioned them. The cops were down here—they talked to them all, too. None of us saw anything but the fire. The fire…then, later, you, carrying your girl out in your arms."

Jennifer glanced over at Brodie. She didn't remember him carrying her out. She'd lost some time from the night before, time she wasn't sure if she'd ever get back, thanks to that blow to the head.

"Search the land. Talk to everyone." Mark waved his hand. "And I'll search with you."

Sometimes, the bonds of friendship could surprise Jennifer. Maybe because she'd never really had a close friend. As Jennifer Wesley, all her friendships had been no more than pretense. And as Jenny Belmont…

She hadn't gotten close to anyone.

Actually, the person who knew her best…that person was Brodie. Did he even realize that?

"There's something else you should know," Brodie said slowly to Mark. "We think that the guy we're after may have a link to my parents' death."

Mark stiffened. "Was he the one who killed them? Who went after Ava?" And suddenly his voice was shaking with fury, a fury that blazed in his eyes.

"We don't know…yet." Brodie seemed to be very

careful with his words as he added, "He has answers we want."

"Then those are the answers we'll get." Mark motioned toward the land again. "Let's start searching."

"Is…is Ava in danger?"

They'd been searching the ranch for more than two hours when Mark finally asked that question. Jennifer was a few feet away, talking with two of the ranch hands. Mark's voice had been pitched so low that Brodie knew she hadn't overheard him.

Mark never liked for anyone to hear him talk about Ava. The guy actually thought he was hiding his feelings pretty well. He was wrong. Brodie knew exactly how his friend felt about Ava.

One day, there's going to be trouble.

Mark was his friend, but Ava…Ava was his baby sister.

"She's safe," Brodie said. "I called her before we left the ranch. She's finishing up her classes at the university then—"

"Is she coming home?"

Brodie shook his head. "You know this isn't home to her any longer."

Mark was silent a bit too long. Then he cleared his throat and said, "So Ava has started a new life." He nodded quickly. "That's good. She…she should be happy. Safe." His gaze turned distant. "When she came to me that night, I couldn't make her stop shaking. No matter what I said or what I did, I couldn't ease her terror."

Brodie started to speak but then stopped.

"What?" Mark demanded.

He shook his head.

"If it's about Ava, you *tell me*." Mark was suddenly right in his path. "If she's—"

"She can't let it go. She still wakes up, screaming at night."

The color bled from Mark's face.

"She's terrified. She thinks the killers will come after her one day." But it wasn't just the terror that was eating up his sister and turning her into a ghost of the person she'd been. "Ava blames herself. She thinks she should have saved our parents. That she should have stayed at the ranch. Fought their attackers."

"She would have died," Mark said, the words hollow. Cold.

But his words were also right.

Mark yanked a hand through his hair. "I need to see her."

"I don't know if that's such a good idea." To Ava, Mark was a constant reminder of the worst night of her life.

Mark's jaw clenched. "I've played by the McGuire rules. I kept my distance—"

"Mark…"

"No more." Said flatly. "You should have told me that she was hurting."

Why? Mark couldn't wave a magic wand and take away Ava's pain. No one could. "There's nothing we can do to stop the pain for her! Not until we catch those men—"

"There's nothing *you* can do," Mark said as his jaw hardened. "But maybe there's something *I* can do."

He didn't like the look in Mark's eyes. "Watch your step," he warned his friend. "That's my sister you're talking about."

"And she's my—"

"What's going on?" Jennifer asked. "What's wrong?"

Mark huffed out a hard breath. "Brodie thinks he can keep me from something I need. He's wrong. Friend or not…he's *wrong*." Then he spun away.

"Uh, okay…" Jennifer put her hands on her hips and faced Brodie. "Want to clue me in about what's happening here?"

"You know my sister was at the ranch when our parents were killed." His gaze was on Mark's tense retreating back. "She fled that night. Saddled up Lady and rode like hell to the only person she felt safe with…"

Jennifer glanced over her shoulder. "Mark."

Yes, Mark. Mark who was Brodie's age…one of Brodie's oldest friends.

Mark had always treated Ava like a kid sister, until that night.

That night had changed so much.

"Mark isn't a safe man." Brodie knew all about the darkness inside him. "And Ava...she's too close to shattering. He needs to stay away from her." He took a step forward, intending to stop Mark.

Jennifer put her hand on his chest. "Maybe you don't know what she needs."

"I know—"

"You can't control everyone, Brodie. You can't control them, and you can't protect them."

But he'd already failed Ava once. He wouldn't, couldn't fail her again.

"It wasn't on you." Jennifer seemed to read his thoughts.

Suddenly feeling too exposed, he tried to turn from her. She caught his arms and turned him right back around. "It wasn't your fault. You didn't let them die. You didn't bring that nightmare into your sister's life. But that's what you've always thought, isn't it?"

He didn't answer her.

"Now...do you think it was my fault?" Her hand slipped from him. "I think Davis does. I could see it in his eyes when we were on the bluff."

"I don't think it's your fault."

She stared up at him. There were emotions he couldn't read in her dark eyes as she said, "And I don't think it's yours." Soft. "So let that guilt go 'cause I believe it's eating you up, just like it's doing to your sister."

Damn. "Heard that part, did you?"

She nodded.

He glanced away from her, toward the line of trees on the right. "Sometimes I don't think—"

He saw it. The sharp edge of a knife, tossed down in the dirt.

"Brodie?"

He hurried forward and bent down. The knife had been dropped near the side of a tree. He wondered if the attacker even knew that he'd lost his weapon. He could have been so hell-bent on his escape that he hadn't realized he'd left the knife behind.

Your mistake.

He picked it up carefully. He could get Shayne to run a fingerprint check on the knife. Then they'd finally know exactly who they were after.

WHILE THE COPS collected the knife and Detective Shayne Townsend started the fingerprint check, Brodie took a protesting Jennifer back to the hospital.

"I'm fine," she said for what Brodie was pretty sure was the fifth time. "I don't need the doctor to poke at me anymore!"

They were alone in the elevator. He narrowed his eyes on her. The woman looked sexy even when she was furious. "The doctor told me I had to bring you back in for a checkup. You know that."

"Fine." Her sigh was long and suffering. "But he's just going to shine a light in my eyes and then push me out of his office. This little visit will be a total waste of time."

He caged her between his body and the elevator wall. "All I need is for him to give me the all clear."

"Brodie?"

"I need to know you're all right." Her scent…seductive, sweet…wrapped around him. "Because I need you."

Her breath caught.

"I know the world is going to hell around us," he said. "I should be holding tight to my control, and the last thing you want is for me to—"

"You're the first thing I want."

The elevator dinged. He heard the doors open behind them, but he didn't step away from her. Right then, he wasn't sure he could move.

"The only thing," she told him, voice soft and sensual.

At that moment, he could have devoured her.

His fingers laced with hers. He lifted her hand and pressed a kiss to her knuckles. "You're the only one I want."

HE WATCHED THEM, slouching in the waiting area as they hurried into the back with the doctor.

Brodie McGuire was far too close to Jennifer. Holding her hand, his body all but surrounding her, protecting her, possessing her.

Jennifer had always been good at using her beauty to captivate men. It had been a talent, one she hadn't even realized that she'd possessed, not at first.

He almost pitied Brodie McGuire. The man didn't understand he was just the latest in a long line of disposable beaus that Jennifer picked up.

Jennifer never formed attachments. After watching her for so long, he wasn't sure that she could.

His phone rang, and he lifted it to his ear.

"Do you see them?" the rasping voice on the other end of the line demanded.

"They're with the doctor now." He'd known that if he just waited, Jennifer would show herself. "I told you," he said to the caller, his voice soft, "I would handle this."

"Because you know what will happen if you fail…"

A nurse glanced over at him. He forced a smile. Like Jennifer, he was good at lies. Deception. He'd even taught her a few of his skills, back in the old days.

"I'll call when it's time for you to come and get her," he answered quietly. Then he ended the call, rose from his seat and slowly headed for the elevator.

There was no point in waiting upstairs. The hunt would begin below, away from all the prying eyes at that hospital.

"Are you happy now?" Jennifer asked quietly as Brodie opened the SUV door for her. "The doctor said I was fine."

Hell, yes, that made him happy. "Damn near delirious with joy," he said and was rewarded with her quick laugh.

He slammed the door. The sound seemed to echo in the parking garage. His gaze raked the area before he climbed into the driver's seat. He pushed the key into the ignition.

"Can I…be with you tonight?" Her laughter was gone.

As always, with her, his desire was strong.

"Back in the elevator, I meant what I said," Jennifer told him.

His head turned toward her. "So did I."

She licked her lips, a nervous gesture but one that he found incredibly sexy. The things he wanted to do with her mouth, *to* her mouth…

"Wrong time, wrong place," she whispered. "I wish I'd come back to you before the danger hit me."

His hand sank into the thickness of her hair. He pulled her toward him. "The danger will pass." *And the time will be right.*

He kissed her. Savored her. There was something about her taste that got to him each time their lips touched. Just something about…her. Need and a white-hot lust surged within him. The more he was with her, the more he had of her, the more Brodie wanted.

He wondered if he would ever get enough of her.

The danger will pass.

He pulled away to stare into her eyes. And knew he would have her soon.

The sun was setting when he pulled out of the parking garage. He knew he'd be back at the ranch before full nightfall hit. Brodie drove them through the city, searching to the left and the right, looking for any signs of danger.

They hadn't gone very far when Brodie realized they were being followed. His gaze kept drifting to the rearview mirror, then to his driver's-side mirror as he studied that other car. At first, the car hung back, staying behind another vehicle. But then the driver became more aggressive.

The vehicle was a small gray four-door. Nothing flashy, nothing that would ever attract attention. And if Brodie hadn't been on alert, maybe he wouldn't have noticed the vehicle.

But he did notice it.

Deliberately, he turned right, testing the other driver.

The gray car turned right.

"I keep thinking about last night," Jennifer said, voice pensive. "Trying to figure out *who* that man is. He knows me, so I should know him."

Brodie turned left.

So did the gray car.

"He said he went to hell because of me," Jennifer whispered. "That I lured him in, turned on him…"

The gray car had pulled up even closer.

"I worked to gather intel," Jennifer continued. "The lifestyle I led gave me special access to my targets. We were hunting high-profile criminals, people who thought they were beyond the reach of the law because they had money and power—"

"We have company," he said, cutting through her words.

"What?"

"Behind us."

She didn't turn around, a good thing, because that move might have tipped off the guy behind them.

"The gray car?" Jennifer asked, and he knew she'd spotted the guy in her mirror.

"Make sure that seat belt is secure," Brodie told her because he had a plan. He grabbed his phone and made a fast call.

Brodie knew the area. As soon as he'd realized that they were being tailed, he'd altered course. They weren't heading to the ranch. They were heading straight to McGuire Securities. *I won't drive into your trap. You'll drive into mine.*

"Open the glove box," he told Jennifer. "Get my gun."

She yanked open the glove box.

The gray car was still following behind them. Obviously, the driver thought he hadn't been spotted yet. Brodie picked up his speed. He'd have to buy some time for Jennifer and him to vanish.

Because it was after the end of the business day, the street in front of McGuire Securities was deserted. *Perfect.* He spun into the parking garage.

From one garage to another...

He parked and rushed out with Jennifer. He took the gun from her, held it tightly. They hunched behind a thick cement column. Lights flashed as the gray car followed them inside the garage.

The driver stopped and jumped from his car.

So eager to come in for the kill? That eagerness would work against the guy.

Brodie shifted his position a bit as he glanced around the column. The driver of that gray car had a baseball cap pulled over his head, and he wore a thick, bulky jacket. *In this Texas heat?* The guy was approaching Brodie's parked vehicle. The SUV's windows were tinted, so he was leaning in close, trying to see inside.

The man had a gun in his hand, a gun that he was keeping near his side.

"Jennifer?" the man called. "I need—"

Brodie attacked. He jumped out from behind the column and went in fast and hard. His approach was silent, deadly, and before the guy could even see him, Brodie had slammed the man, stomach-first, into the side of the vehicle.

The man's gun fell to the ground. Brodie pushed his weapon into the guy's back. "You should have run away," Brodie snarled. "You should have *never* come after her again!"

"Wait!" the man yelled. "You've got the wrong idea!"

The fellow's voice was cracking with fear… The voice was also different…not the same guy that Brodie had confronted at the Montgomery ranch.

"Brodie!" Jennifer cried out.

He glanced toward her. She'd run from behind the column and she'd picked up the gun.

The stranger's head turned toward her, too.

"Damn straight," the guy seemed to *encourage* her. "Keep that weapon on him, Jennifer. Don't let him hurt me! I'm here to help you. *You know that!* I've always helped you!"

Help her?

"Brodie, that's not the man who has been stalking me."

Brodie spun the guy around. The man's baseball hat fell off and hit the cement.

"That's Nate Wesley," she continued as she took a few steps forward. Her voice was shocked. "He's the agent who was assigned the role of my father."

Her supposedly dead father.

Hell.

Chapter Eight

Jennifer couldn't believe she was staring at Nate. He should have been so far away, living a nice, safe, *normal* life.

Instead, Brodie had his gun against his chest, and Nate's face was a picture of fear.

"I saw this guy take you from the hospital," Nate said. "I thought he was going to hurt you—"

"I'm protecting her." Brodie's face and voice were just scary.

"How was I supposed to know that?" Nate's voice rose, then cracked. "You came out, nearly running with her. You put her in your ride and you hightailed it out of there."

They had been in a hurry to leave. Mostly because Brodie had been afraid the stalker might be watching them. Sighing, Jennifer lowered the gun in her hand. "Brodie, it's okay. He's not a threat."

Brodie didn't budge. "I'm not so sure of that." His words were a snarl. "Why were you even at the hospital? How did you know Jennifer was in Austin? Why are you here?"

Nate flinched. He looked older…so much older. The lines on his face were deeper, and the gray at his temples had spread to streak through his dark brown hair. "I heard about what happened in New Orleans. The fire at Jennifer's place made the news. I went to check on her, and I followed her trail to Austin."

"You're lying," Brodie said flatly.

"No, no, I'm not! I wanted to help her! We worked together for years. You think I'd just turn my back on her if I thought she was in danger? I was worried, so I followed her. When I got to Austin, I remembered that you'd worked that rescue mission in the Middle East. I remembered the way Jennifer had been so determined to pay you back…"

Nate had been the one to connect her with Brodie's parents. He'd pulled strings and gotten their address for her. Since he'd been so involved, yes, Nate *would* have made the connection between her and Brodie once he'd gotten to Austin.

"She changed after that mission… We both did," Nate added quietly.

Jennifer crept forward. She still had the weapon in her hand, but she wasn't aiming it at anyone. "Brodie, he's not a threat."

"I'm not so sure of that." Brodie didn't look toward her. "He's here, following us…at the hospital—"

"Since I got to town, I've been listening to the police scanner," Nate told him, body tensing. "I heard about the big fire at the Montgomery ranch. About the woman who was brought into the hospital. I knew the Montgomery property was near the McGuire ranch—"

"And how did you know that?"

"Because he's the one who led me to your parents years ago." Her left hand wrapped around Brodie's arm. "Please, lower the gun."

Brodie finally looked her in the eyes. "You really trust this man? With your life?"

"I—"

"With mine?"

Jennifer frowned. She looked down at the gun in her right hand. Nate's gun. Nate had been following her, and he'd been armed. If he truly meant no threat, then why the weapon? Just for his protection? Or for something more...

Nate had been so adept at lying in the field. He'd gotten the deadliest of criminals to trust him within a matter of moments.

He'd taught Jennifer how to lie.

Brodie exhaled and stepped back. "Fine, have it your way..."

And she saw Nate lunge away from the vehicle.

Jennifer stepped in his path. She had the gun up and aimed right at her ex-mentor in less than two seconds' time. "No," Jennifer said softly. "I don't trust him with your life."

Then something happened. She'd stared into Nate's eyes dozens of times. She'd thought that she could see right past the mask that he usually wore when dealing with others.

But she'd been wrong. Because this time, in *this* moment, she finally did see him for the man that he was.

His eyes hardened. His face tightened with fury. "I won't die for you," he shouted at Jennifer. "You're going down, but you won't take me with you!"

She shook her head. "Nate?"

"He's coming." He laughed, and the laughter echoed around them in that empty garage. "I called him. Told him where we were going for every second of that ride. You think you trapped me in here? He's got you now. You and your lover. He'll kill you both!"

Footsteps pounded then as men rushed from the darkness.

Only…

These were McGuires. Not her stalker. Not the man Nate had just said would come to kill her and Brodie.

"We called someone during the ride, too," Brodie murmured. "And just so you know…no one's dying tonight."

THEY TOOK NATE WESLEY—or, the man known as Nate Wesley—into the McGuire Securities office. Grant and Sullivan kept a tight hold on him. Sullivan…this had been her first encounter with the youngest McGuire brother. For some reason, she'd expected him to be a bit softer than his siblings. He wasn't. If anything, he seemed even harder, even more dangerous. A deadly intensity clung to him like a second skin.

Jennifer didn't go into that office with them. She retreated to the bathroom as she tried to settle her ragged nerves. When she stared at her reflection in the mirror, Jennifer hardly recognized the woman with the haunted eyes and pale cheeks.

Nate came to betray me.

She'd trusted him, worked side by side with him for so long. She'd been trying to protect him, but he'd been in the hunt for her all along. It was really true… Her former life had been nothing but a lie.

Her fingers tightened around the edge of the sink. She wasn't going to let Nate see her tears. She wasn't going to let him see her pain at all. So she stood in that bathroom, and she didn't make a sound as the tears fell. Those tears…they were for the friend she'd *thought* she had. They were for the life that had been hers for too many years…a life that was dead and buried now.

When the tears were done, she swiped her hands

over her cheeks. Her eyes gleamed in the mirror. *There's still too much pain there.*

She pinched her cheeks, trying to bring back some color. *Never let them see your weakness.*

That had been Nate's advice, the first day that she'd been paired with him. She'd been so nervous. Her legs had been shaking like crazy. But he'd smiled at her, tapped her on the chin. Told her...

We're in this together. An old pro and a rookie... They'll never see us coming.

And they hadn't.

Just as... *I hadn't seen Nate's betrayal coming.*

"Jennifer?" Brodie called. A light rap sounded on the door. "Are you all right?"

"Fine." Her voice was too flat, but at least it didn't tremble. One more swipe of her hands over her cheeks, and then Jennifer turned away from her reflection.

Her head was pounding as Jennifer opened the bathroom door. Brodie was waiting in the hallway, and he straightened when he saw her. "You okay?"

No. She wanted to collapse some place, but Jennifer made herself nod. "I'm fine."

"The hell you are." Then he was wrapping his arms around her and holding her tightly. She wanted to sink into him and pretend the nightmare around her wasn't real.

But it is. And I can't escape from it.

"You don't have to go in there," he said as his

arms tightened around her. "Grant and Sullivan can handle the interrogation. They've got backup coming. I called in Shayne Townsend."

Shayne, right, he was the Austin police detective that she knew Brodie had contacted before.

"He'll be here within twenty minutes—"

"I need to talk with Nate." She pulled back as she stared up into his eyes. "I have to face him." She'd face Nate and his betrayal head-on, even if it ripped out her heart. "I can get to him—I know I can."

Brodie's face was grim. "He wants you dead."

Apparently, there was a line of people who did. She eased away from him and immediately missed the reassuring warmth of his body. "He's not getting what he wants." But she *would* get her answers. "He knows the man who is after me. I'll get him to talk. I'll get him to tell me everything he knows."

"You'll play nice with him—is that it?" Brodie asked her.

No, there wasn't going to be anything nice about what was coming.

"Fine," he said softly. "But if he doesn't talk, then my brothers and I will get our turn with him. I assure you, there won't be anything nice about the way we play."

She believed him.

Brodie shook his head. "You're trembling."

Nate betrayed me. When would the pain from that blow lessen?

But how she felt didn't matter. It couldn't matter, not then. She and Brodie both needed to be safe. They needed the threat gone. "I want to talk with him now," she whispered as she stared up into Brodie's eyes.

His sigh was rough. "Fine. But you need to know…whatever he says in there, whatever he reveals, you're safe, got it? I will be with you every moment, and I need you to know that you're safe… with me."

Her hand lifted, pressed lightly to the stubble that lined his jaw. "I already do know that." Why else would she have come to Austin in the first place? She'd always felt safe with Brodie. He was the one who shouldn't feel safe with her.

"I'm staying by your side," he told her, voice gruff. "Every moment," he said once more.

"That sounds like a good idea to me." By her side—that was exactly where she wanted him to be.

"First, though," Brodie muttered, "I need this." And he kissed her. A soft, light caress of his lips against hers.

Tears stung her eyes again. She leaned into him, let that kiss linger. Her lips parted beneath his, and Brodie deepened the kiss. He seemed to savor her, and she just needed him. So much. The kiss had passion, but it also had…more. Emotion seemed to swell in the air around her, and there was a tenderness, a care to his touch that had her whole body tightening.

When he pulled back, his hand lifted. The back of his hand slid over her cheek. "I don't like to see you cry."

She hadn't realized that the tears had escaped. She should have been more careful, but she'd been lost in him for a moment. "Brodie…"

A door opened down the hallway. Grant stuck his head out and frowned at them. "Are you two all right?"

She was shattering on the inside, but Jennifer managed, "Yes." Brodie was at her side as they walked down that hallway and as they headed into Grant's office.

Nate had been handcuffed to a chair. He sat there, glaring at her when she walked into the room. Grant moved to stand on Nate's left. Sullivan, looking like an even rougher, angrier version of Brodie, stood positioned at Nate's right.

"You're going to let them do this to me?" Nate shouted at her as he yanked at his cuffs. Each wrist was handcuffed to the chair. "After all I did for you?"

Brodie was right at her side, just as he'd said he would be. "What you did for me?" Jennifer repeated, head shaking. "We worked together because we were assigned that job." She tried to take slow, even breaths. Tried to look as though she were controlled, when really her heart was racing like mad in her chest.

"I could have let them kill you in the Middle East! I'm the one who called in the favors. I'm the one who got lover boy over there—" Nate's eyes flashed at Brodie "—to go in and save you."

Brodie's shoulders rolled. "That's lie number one."

Nate tensed.

"We've been doing some digging of our own," Grant murmured, never moving from his guard position near Nate. "You see…we have quite a few government contacts, too."

Jennifer didn't know if Brodie and Grant were bluffing or not, but the quick break in Nate's expression told her plenty. Her stomach knotted. "You didn't want to save me. You wanted to save yourself. You were afraid that my captors might break me, and I'd tell them about you."

He glanced away from her.

"I wouldn't have done that to you," she whispered, and the words were the absolute truth. "I would have protected you."

His gaze was directed just over her shoulder. *He won't look me in the eyes.* "Nate!"

He jerked. "You don't know what you'd do if the right pressure was applied. No one ever knows, not until it's too late."

She stepped toward him. "Is that what's happening? Is someone applying pressure to you now?"

There were monitors to the right of Grant. Security feeds that showed different interior and exterior shots of the building. She saw Grant glance over at them. A man had just appeared in the feed on the lower right.

"Detective Townsend is here," Grant said with a slight roll of his shoulders. "Sullivan, go let him in."

Sullivan gave a curt nod and slid from the room.

Nate laughed. "A cop? What's a cop going to do? I haven't broken any laws! He can't do a thing to me!"

Brodie's glittering stare raked Nate. "You're working with the man after Jennifer. You already admitted that you called him."

Only the guy pulling Nate's strings must have realized that they weren't falling for his trap. He hadn't shown at the parking garage.

Nate's mouth clamped closed. Then his lips twisted. "There a law against making a phone call?"

Brodie took a step toward him. Jennifer put her hand on Brodie's arm, stopping him. Her gaze stayed focused on Nate. "Talk to me," Jennifer told him. "Tell me how things got so twisted."

Nate shook his head.

"You're supposed to be married. You and Shelly… you were going to start a new life together. Settle down, forget everything that had passed before. You were going to be *free*. We both were." Shelly had been one of their government handlers. She'd wanted out, too, and she'd retired from the business with Nate. Jennifer had thought those two were really in love.

His jaw hardened. "I'm not talking about Shelly."

That knot in her stomach got worse. "What happened?"

No answer.

"Nate!" She wanted to grab him. Shake him. "Why would you sell me out?" Then she remembered what he'd said to her in that parking garage. *I won't die for you.* "He came after you," she whispered. "Did he come to kill you? Is that what happened? Did he track you down and try to kill you first?"

His eyelids flickered, and Jennifer knew she was right.

"It's someone we put away, isn't it? He blamed you, just like he blamed me. Only…he came after you *first*."

Nate turned his attention to the shut office door. "The cop isn't going to do anything to me."

Her head tilted. "Where is Shelly?"

He flinched.

"Nate…*where's Shelly*?"

The door opened. She turned her head. Saw a tall, broad-shouldered man with sandy-blond hair follow Sullivan into the room. A badge was clipped to the man's belt. The guy took one look at the scene before him and froze.

"Please, *please* tell me there's a reason that man is handcuffed."

But Nate wasn't looking his way. Nate's head had sagged forward. "Shelly's gone."

Chill bumps rose on Jennifer's arms.

"He wanted me to suffer. Said I deserved it because of what I'd done." Nate's breath heaved out. "There was a fire…"

Her hands gripped his shoulders. "Nate, you should have contacted me!"

He shook his head. "She was gone in an instant, and he said I'd be next…if I didn't give him you."

Her hands tightened on him. She needed him to look up at her. "That's how he knew I was in New Orleans. You told him I was down there."

"What is going on?" The detective demanded.

Jennifer's gaze jerked toward him.

"This man—" Brodie glared at Nate "—is working with a killer. The man who set that Mustang to blow, the man who torched the Montgomery stables."

Nate started to laugh. "The man who is going to kill Jennifer."

Jennifer backed away from him.

"The hell he is," Brodie said, voice lethal.

Nate cocked his head as he seemed to study

Brodie. "Is your family worth her life? Because that's what the choice is going to be. He won't stop."

"Who is he?" Jennifer asked. "Give me his name."

Nate laughed. "You don't even remember him. Neither did I at first. All the people we worked to put away, and he's the one who comes gunning for us? Sure never saw that coming, not until it was too late."

She needed the guy's *name*. "His voice was familiar."

"I think he was falling for you," Nate said, nodding a bit. "Maybe that's why he went off the deep end. He thought you were perfect…that you were going to be his…and then he realized you were stealing his secrets."

Jennifer stiffened. And the pieces clicked for her. Because there had been only one man that she'd walked the line with during her years as an agent. One man that she'd thought, *Maybe he's innocent,* but then the evidence had shown just how guilty he really was. Just how evil. Her blinders had come off just in time. "Stephen?" She barely breathed the name. Stephen Brushard.

Nate laughed again. "I'm dead now. You realize that, right?"

"Okay," the detective barked, and he strode forward with sudden aggression. "We're taking this downtown. We're talking murders…espionage… This is going downtown."

Brodie caught Jennifer's arm. "Who's Stephen?"

She opened her mouth to reply—

But Nate beat her to the punch. "Rich boy, psychotic killer."

Jennifer wet her lips. "He was...he was the first case I worked. I was so scared. Didn't even think I could pull off being...*her*."

Brodie frowned at that.

"Stephen Brushard was an American businessman with suspected ties to the Russian mob. It was believed that he was providing them with drugs, with weapons, but on paper he seemed so clean." On paper and in person. He'd been so charming, so caring. She'd never had a man like him show any interest in her. As Jenny Belmont, no one had been interested in anything about her.

Stephen had been different. He'd been her assignment, but Jennifer knew he'd become more. She'd even gone to Nate in those early days and told him that she thought they were after the wrong guy. Stephen had to be innocent.

No one's innocent. Nate's reply had been flat. *You'll learn that truth soon enough.*

And with Stephen, she had.

"They always do look good on paper," Nate muttered. "That's what covers are for. Then you rip past those lies and you see that *no one* has clean hands. They're all stained with blood."

She pulled in a quick breath and kept her focus

on Brodie. "Stephen took an interest in me. I...I got access to his computer. Personal files." That was when she'd learned the truth about him. She'd actually thought those files might exonerate him, but...they'd just nailed the coffin shut on his case. She'd learned about the monster hiding behind the man's face. "I found out about an upcoming drop. I tipped off our handlers, and Stephen was caught in the act." And Prince Charming had been locked up.

Nate yanked at his cuffs once more. "Prisons in Russia aren't exactly known as paradise."

The US agents had been working with their Russian counterparts. The bust had gone down so easily—almost too easily. And she'd been out of the country even before the bust had been made. "Stephen shouldn't have known I was the one involved." They'd been so careful. Her gaze slid back toward Nate. "We both should have been covered."

Nate shrugged—or shrugged as much as he could in those cuffs. "The guy was smart. He put the puzzle pieces together... Guess he had plenty of time to figure things out while he was rotting in that Russian cell."

And now Stephen wanted her to suffer, just as he had.

"Our cover is blown," Nate said grimly. "And even my supposed death couldn't stop him from finding me."

But it should have stopped Stephen. With his

"death," Nate had more protection than she'd been given. A new name, a new identity. Yet Stephen had found him. *How?* Did Stephen have government contacts? Sources that had turned on her and Nate?

Grant and Sullivan had been watching the interrogation in silence, but now Grant stepped forward. A frown had pulled his brows low. "You said you called him," Grant said, "and we found your smashed phone right outside of the parking garage."

Nate swallowed. "Stephen told me to get rid of the phone and wait for him."

Grant's eyes narrowed on the man. "But you have his number. *You* called him." A brief pause. "And you're going to do it again."

Frantically, Nate shook his head. "No way, that's not happening. You think I'm going to set that guy up? After what he did to Shelly?"

"You should do it *because* of what he did to Shelly," Jennifer nearly yelled at him. "Stephen has to be stopped!"

"Downtown," Detective Shayne Townsend muttered again. "We are taking this mess downtown. Where are the handcuff keys?"

"He's not leaving," Brodie said, voice lethal, "not until he makes that call." He stalked toward Nate, leaned forward until they were eye level. "You think this Stephen Brushard is scary? Wait until you have me and all of my brothers gunning for you."

"You can't say things like that!" the detective nearly shouted.

Brodie ignored him. "I'm betting you did some digging on me. On my family. You might even know about some of our missions."

Nate's Adam's apple bobbed.

"You *will* make that call," Brodie said, "or you'll be dealing with us…and the hell that we will bring to you."

Nate's gaze flew to her. "Jennifer, come on. For old times' sake, *help me*."

Old times' sake… Had he really just gone there? "You were going to let him kill me, weren't you?" Not just her, though. In that garage, he'd been prepared to attack Brodie.

"Uh…" She could practically see the wheels turning in his head as he tried to figure out what lie to tell her.

"The old times are over." She glared at him. "Now make the call."

"WHAT ARE YOU THINKING? *Are* you thinking?" Detective Shayne Townsend demanded as he grabbed Brodie and hauled him into the hallway. "You can't threaten to kill a man right in front of me! Damn it, does the badge I wear mean nothing to you McGuires anymore?"

Brodie sucked in a hard breath and held tightly to his control. "It still means something. That's why we called you and didn't just go after this killer, Stephen Brushard, on our own."

Shayne yanked a hand through his hair. "What have I walked into here? Sullivan only gave me skeleton details…"

"Because we were still walking in the dark ourselves." And he wanted to hurry back into that room with Grant, Jennifer, Sullivan and dear old Nate to find out more. "All right, yeah, you know Jennifer was being stalked. Well, less than an hour ago, we learned that Nate in there is working for the guy."

"And who the hell is Nate?"

"An ex-government agent." He hesitated, then said, "Just like Jennifer. The guy was her partner in the field, but they both got out of the business years ago."

Shayne squeezed his eyes shut. "Spies."

"*Ex*-spies."

Shayne swore. "Do you know the kind of paperwork we're talking?"

"Nate is a puppet on a string. We have to pull in Brushard before that guy strikes again." His muscles were locked down. "Before he kills Jennifer."

"Wait—just *wait*." Shayne's expression turned pensive. "Have you gotten official confirmation that those two were spies? I mean, I know you have contacts in the government—have they backed up the woman's story? How do you know you can actually trust what she's saying? What *he's* saying?"

"Grant is getting confirmation."

Shayne's sigh was loud and long. "And in the meantime, that Nate guy is just going to—what? Call in some killer who will waltz right up to us and turn himself in?"

No way would it be that easy. "I'd expect more of a fight. That's why we want your boys in blue here."

Shayne's shoulders sagged. "Being friends with the McGuires is never easy."

Brodie waited.

"He makes the call," Shayne finally said, "but that only happens at the PD. Where we can monitor him, where *my* men can trace the call and be lead on this investigation."

No, this wasn't—

"You and your brothers aren't vigilantes, Brodie. You can't just keep a man handcuffed, no matter what he's done." Shayne jutted out his chin. "I'm taking him downtown. I have to do it—that's my job. You and your brothers follow us. Then we'll bring in the killer out there who's gunning for your girl." Shayne's gaze was troubled. "You knew you were walking the line on this one already, didn't you? That's why you called me in. Not because you wanted backup."

"The jerk nearly killed Mark Montgomery." And when Brodie thought of Jennifer's stalker, a killing rage coursed through him. Maybe he was worried about crossing the line because for Jennifer... *I'd do it.*

Shayne nodded. "We're going to stop him, but we have to do it the *right* way." And then Shayne marched back into Grant's office, and Brodie followed on his heels.

"Uncuff him," Shayne ordered when he stood right in front of Nate.

Grant didn't move. Neither did Sullivan.

"I'm taking him into custody."

Nate's eyes widened. "On what charge? I didn't do anything." His cheeks flushed a dark red. "I'm the victim! I'm the one they kidnapped and handcuffed! You need to be arresting those fools!"

"Maybe if he hadn't heard you raging in here, he would have bought your innocent act more," Grant muttered.

Shayne's jaw hardened. "Uncuff him. Now."

Sullivan glanced at Grant. Grant looked at Brodie.

Jennifer frowned at them all.

"Stop the silent McGuire communication," Shayne snapped. "My department will give you full backing to track down this Stephen Brushard. But we're doing it the right way. And this guy...he's getting put in a cell."

Brodie nodded at Grant. Grant pulled the keys from his pocket. He unhooked the cuffs. Before Nate could jump out of his chair, Shayne had pulled out his weapon and the detective aimed it right at the ex-agent. "I'm following the law. Don't mistake that for weakness on my part. You make any move to attack me or the McGuires, and you will regret it. I promise you that." He motioned with his gun. "Now, stand up and keep your hands behind your back. You're getting cuffed again—because I don't want to worry about you trying to attack me."

Nate's glare should have burned the flesh right off Shayne.

When Nate was up and his hands were cuffed behind his back, the guy's face turned an even darker red. "Do you know who I am?" He demanded as his white-hot stare raked Shayne. "You can't do this to me!"

"Give it a rest, Nate," Jennifer muttered. "They don't care who you were or who you are… They're taking you in." Brodie hated the sadness in her eyes. She'd trusted Nate, but he'd sold her out.

Shayne pulled Nate forward. "Come on, my car's waiting outside."

Grant and Sullivan followed behind him. Jennifer started to advance, but Brodie blocked her path. "Are you okay?" he asked, keeping his voice low.

Her lips trembled, but then she pressed them together and gave a quick nod.

"Jennifer?"

"I… We worked together for so long. I think I might have even started to pretend to myself…

thinking that we were *some* kind of family." Her lashes lowered, shielding her eyes. "I would never have sold him out. I guess…I guess you really can't depend on anyone but yourself, huh?"

His fingers cupped her chin. "You can depend on me." He needed her to know that. To understand. Whatever came their way, he was going to be at her side.

"Do you mean that?"

Hell, yes, he did.

Her breath rushed out. "Thank you."

He wanted to take her into his arms, to hold her tight, but the danger wasn't over. They had more work to do. And now that they had the PD behind them, that work would go a hell of a lot faster.

"Come on," he said, and they headed for the door.

Sullivan was the first one to exit the building. He went out, sweeping the area. The cameras had shown no sign that any intruder was close by, but since Nate said he'd tipped off Stephen, they didn't want to take any chances.

Grant left next, armed, body tense.

Shayne pulled Nate out. Nate was digging in his heels. Twisting his arms. "I'm not telling you anything!" His voice rose. "I've already lost too much! I won't lose anything else! I won't!"

Brodie followed closely behind Shayne. Jennifer was at his side. Brodie's gaze swept the scene.

Shayne's vehicle was just a few feet away. There was no sign of Stephen.

Because he got tipped off and ran...but we'll pull him in again. We won't lose him.

Shayne shoved Nate into the back of his car. Then he looked over at Sullivan. "Will you—"

"I'll make sure the guy doesn't cause any trouble." Sullivan climbed into Shayne's car.

Shayne nodded. "Good. Then let's get out of here."

They loaded into the vehicles and headed out.

Grant was in the lead vehicle. Shayne and Sullivan were driving in the second car with Nate. Brodie took the protective cover as the last in their line.

"We're going to have Brushard in custody soon," Brodie told Jennifer. He risked a fast glance at her. She looked so fragile. So tired as she sat beside him in that car.

"I was just doing my job," she murmured. "I saw the evidence against him. He'd destroyed so many lives…" He heard the faint click of her swallow. "I had to turn him in, and now Stephen is trying to destroy me."

He caught her hand. Held tight. "That's not happening." Not on his watch.

"WHY ARE YOU all willing to die for her?" The man known as Nate Wesley asked as he leaned forward.

Sullivan glared at the guy. He didn't trust him for an instant.

"I mean, Brodie, I get that part. They're lovers, right? Have to be." Nate exhaled. "So she's got him wrapped up tight, but you two guys? I mean, come on… You don't want to get in Stephen Brushard's way. Believe me, you *don't*."

Shayne kept his eyes on the road.

Sullivan knew the detective wanted Nate to keep talking—to keep digging his own grave with every word he said. Sullivan knew, because he wanted the exact same thing.

"You're scared of the guy," Sullivan muttered.

"He killed my Shelly!" Nate snarled. "Of course I'm scared of him. The man escaped a Russian prison. He's got ties so deep with the Russian mob… He's *death*. If you don't give him what he wants, then he'll rip your world to shreds."

Shayne braked at a red light. The street around them was deserted. "And what he wants is Jennifer?"

"He doesn't love her. Those softer feelings are long dead for him." Nate jerked at his cuffs. "He's furious because she betrayed him, and he's an eye-for-an-eye type. He's not going to stop. He won't ever stop, not until he gets what he wants."

Jennifer's death.

Sullivan heard a faint click. He tensed as his gaze sharpened on Nate. "I want you to sit back now."

Nate had leaned forward, perching on the edge of the backseat.

"I won't just wait for the guy to come at me. You think I'll be safe in jail?" Nate's voice rose even more. "He'll get to me! If he thinks I'm betraying him, then he'll kill me just like he's going to kill her!"

Sullivan grabbed for the guy. "I told you to sit—"

Nate's hands flew up. His *uncuffed* hands. Too late, Sullivan realized what that faint click had been. The cuffs dangled loosely from Nate's right hand, and he swung that hand hard at Sullivan's face.

"What's happening back there?" Shayne barked.

Sullivan felt his nose break on impact.

Nate leaped toward the front of the car. He locked his arm around Shayne's neck. The car immediately swerved to the right as Shayne fought him.

Sullivan's hands closed around Nate. "Let him go!" he shouted. Damn, the guy was stronger than he looked. "Let him—"

The car crashed into a light post.

Chapter Nine

Brodie slammed on the brakes and jumped out of his SUV. "Sullivan!" He ran toward Shayne's smashed vehicle, adrenaline and fear eating at him as he roared his brother's name.

Jennifer's footsteps pounded over the pavement as she rushed after him.

The back door opened on Shayne's car. Nate staggered out. He saw Brodie. Jennifer. "They're dead," he shouted as he stilled under a streetlight.

No, no, Sullivan was *not* dead. Up the street, Grant had braked his car, and he was running back toward the wreckage.

Brodie grabbed Nate, his hands locking around the guy's shoulders. "What did you do?" He shook the older man.

Nate smiled. "I wasn't the driver...I'm not the one who killed them."

This guy had been a government agent? "What happened to you?"

Nate's eyelids jerked. "Death. You lose everyone, everything, then you learn to watch out for yourself."

And Brodie felt the hard edge of a knife press into his stomach.

"Your brother had a knife strapped to his ankle." Nate gave a little shrug. "I was always pretty good with knives."

The knife jabbed deeper into Brodie's side.

"I'm not calling Stephen Brushard," Nate said. "And I don't care who I have to kill in order to—"

Brodie grabbed his wrist, shattered the bones. The knife dropped to the ground with a clatter. Brodie shoved Nate back, back, until the guy's shoulders slammed into the side of a brick building.

"If they're dead," Brodie said, his low words a promise, "then so are you."

"You broke my wrist!"

"I'll break more than that if you ever try to hurt my brother or my friend again." Brodie held Nate pinned to the wall. He glanced over his shoulder, trying to see what was happening with the wreckage.

The front of Shayne's car was smashed to hell and back. Glass littered the street. Brodie could see someone slumped in the backseat.

Sullivan.

Jennifer was climbing into the backseat, trying to reach Sullivan, while Grant had yanked open the driver's door in an attempt to get Shayne out of the wreckage.

"He's alive!" Jennifer shouted.

"He won't be for long," Nate whispered. "Stephen Brushard took away the woman I loved because she was in his way. What do you think he'll do to those men? To the cop? To your brother? Is she really worth their lives?"

Shayne stumbled out of the vehicle. No other cars were on that street, not yet. This business area was usually pretty empty on the weekend.

Grant rushed to help Jennifer.

"Choose carefully," Nate told him.

Brodie wanted to drive his fist into the guy's jaw. "She lived as your daughter for years! Don't you care at all about what happens to her?" He let Nate go but didn't back away far. *You're not getting away.*

"All that was a lie. The woman you *think* you know is a lie." Nate stepped away from the wall. "I won't lose everything I have just for—"

A gunshot rang out.

Nate's words ended in a strangled gasp as red ballooned on his chest.

He followed us.

Brodie grabbed Nate and yanked him to the right, trying to give the guy cover. *"Jennifer! Grant!"*

At first, the only sound he heard was the wail of a siren, coming closer. Had Shayne called for backup?

Then… "We're okay!" Jennifer yelled.

Nate definitely wasn't okay. Brodie put his hands on Nate's chest, trying to stop the blood flow, but the shot had been far too accurate.

The bullet had blasted straight into Nate's heart.

Nate's breath heaved out. His head turned toward Brodie. "See…told you…no…escape…"

His eyes closed.

No.

"Where's the shooter?" Grant called.

More gunfire rang out then. More blasts. The bullets slammed right into the car. Brodie looked over and saw that Grant and Jennifer were in the backseat of Shayne's wrecked car. The rear window had just shattered, spilling glass down on them as they curled over Sullivan.

Shayne was behind the wrecked car, trying to take aim up at a building on the right. Brodie caught the glint of a weapon on the third floor.

He didn't follow us. He was waiting for us…

How had the guy known they'd be taking Nate to the police station?

Grant fired back at the shooter, and, using that gunfire as cover, Brodie ran toward the building on the right. The shooter was there…*waiting*. He could get him. But—

Police cruisers rushed up to the scene. Two of them. The cops jumped out and pointed their weapons at Brodie.

"Freeze!" a uniformed cop shouted. "And drop the weapon!"

The weapon? Brodie looked at his hand and saw the knife he'd picked up. *Hell.* Grabbing it had been second nature to him. "Wrong guy," he told them. "I'm not the threat—he's up there!"

"I said drop it!" the cop shouted.

Brodie looked up at the window. He was right out there in the open, a perfect target. So were the cops. If Brushard wanted to take him out, this was the moment. "He can kill us all. You need to get back behind your patrol car. *Now.*"

The cops came closer. "I told you—"

"I'm Detective Shayne Townsend!" Shayne's voice seemed weaker than normal. "Badge 210. I'm the one who radioed in… That man is with me. We've got a shooter upstairs…third floor."

The cops looked toward that window and hurriedly backed up. One called in and confirmed Shayne's badge number.

But they kept their weapons pointed at Brodie.

"He's getting away," Brodie said. The man's getaway had to be the reason why he hadn't fired yet. "We can't just stand here, waiting, while that shooter runs. He just killed a man!"

And those fresh-faced cops weren't equipped to handle the guy. But Brodie was.

"Let me go after him," Brodie snarled.

"No, everyone stay right where you are!" This

shout came from the taller cop, the guy with red hair. "We'll get this sorted out."

"You're letting him get away," Brodie snapped.

"We need an ambulance!" Shayne called out. "Hurry!"

The cops got confirmation on Shayne's badge, and they *finally* sprang into action. One ran toward the wrecked car.

One ran for the building—and Brodie was right behind him.

Brodie rushed up a flight of stairs, even as he heard the scream of more sirens outside. Help, coming in like a fury.

Too late for Nate. But not for Sullivan. *Not for my brother.*

They burst onto the third floor. The cop ran in with a shout, and Brodie had to jerk the guy back. But the third floor was empty, a cavernous open space in the abandoned building.

Damn it. He'd feared the shooter was getting away. When the bullets hadn't torn into him, he'd known that deafening silence had meant that the perp was fleeing.

His hands fisted as he went toward the window on the right. The window that was still open and looked out on the street.

An ambulance was below. More patrol cars. Shayne was directing the scene, and Brodie saw that Sullivan had been pulled from the car.

"The third floor's empty," the cop said, and Brodie glanced back at him. The kid was on his radio. "We'll search all the floors. We need backup!"

Brodie's hand slammed into the window frame. A small chunk of glass fell loose when he hit it. Brodie frowned at that glass. He picked it up. Tilted it.

Light glinted off the glass.

The shooter wasn't here. He was somewhere else... He wasn't here!

Frantic now, his gaze went back to the street below. Jennifer was being pulled away by Shayne. She glanced up toward him, her face etched with fear and—

No!

"Jennifer!" he roared.

Sullivan was on a stretcher. Grant turned at Brodie's shout.

Jennifer was out in the open. Too easy. What was Shayne thinking to let her stand out there like that? Shayne knew she was the guy's target.

"Get cover!" Brodie yelled. "Get—"

Gunfire exploded.

But it didn't hit Jennifer. Grant had grabbed her, and they'd hit the ground.

The sirens screamed again.

"He's in the next building," Brodie yelled. This time, he'd seen exactly where that shot came from. "Not this one! We need men in there before he hurts anyone else!"

Brodie and the fresh-faced cop rushed down the stairs. The scene on the street was chaos as the cops swarmed and hurried to search for the shooter.

Only…

They couldn't find him.

Because even though they searched every room in the nearby building, the shooter was nowhere to be seen.

JENNIFER WASN'T EXACTLY a fan of police stations. Or rather, she didn't enjoy sitting in an interrogation room for hours, being separated from Brodie and being forced to answer the same questions over and over again.

Brodie trusted Shayne Townsend, but it was quickly apparent that Shayne was more than a little suspicious of Jennifer. Not that Jennifer blamed him. He'd known her for a very short time, and, during the few hours of their acquaintance, he'd nearly been killed.

She was kind of a dangerous woman to know.

"I want you to tell me everything you can about Stephen Brushard." Shayne sat across the table, glaring at her.

Weary, so very weary, Jennifer could only shake her head.

Pain knifed through her when she thought of Nate. His body had been bagged and tagged at the scene. Taken away…

Jennifer cleared her throat. "I'm his target."

Shayne's fingers drummed on the table. "Why is this guy longing for your death so much? Tell me everything. Every single detail about your relationship with him."

"I can't." Her shoulders slumped with weariness. "Most of it is classified, and you don't have the clearance to—"

His hands slammed onto the table. "A man was murdered less than ten feet from me! No one brings this kind of danger to my door." His eyes turned to slits as he glared at her. "You think I'm going to stand back and let the McGuires all fall next?"

She shook her head. "The last thing I want is for them to be hurt."

"But they have already been hurt—a great deal." He opened a file and tossed the black-and-white picture toward her. It was the picture that she and Brodie had recovered from the Mustang, the picture of her and Brodie's mother. "Are you tied to the death of Brodie's parents?"

I don't know. Her fingers brushed against the edge of the photograph.

"Was Stephen Brushard the man who killed Brodie's parents?" Shayne demanded.

"I think he was in prison then." She hadn't even realized that he'd escaped. The last she'd heard about Stephen Brushard, he'd been sentenced to twenty years of confinement.

"Then you believe he hired someone?" Shayne pressed. "Because he was so determined to get to you? Is that what happened? He hired someone to—"

"I don't know what happened!" Her breath heaved out. "I want to see Brodie. Is he okay? Is he—"

"Brodie is with Sullivan." He motioned toward the mirror on the right. She knew it was a two-way mirror, but Jennifer didn't know who was watching her from that other room. "They're both in there," Shayne said, as if reading her thoughts, "watching you."

What? Instinctively, she shook her head.

"Brodie didn't take kindly to the fact that his baby brother got caught in your cross fire. I mean, sure, Sullivan's an ex-Marine, but there's getting hurt in battle, and then there's getting hurt for no damn reason at all."

Her breath hitched. Brodie was just watching Shayne interrogate her?

"The thing is," Shayne continued softly, "I can't find any records about your so-called involvement with the government. Grant can't get confirmation. No one can back up your story—"

"No one will back it up." That wasn't how these situations worked. "I was a ghost agent." So deep undercover that only a few higher-ups at the CIA even knew about her. Those higher-ups would never confirm her identity.

Shayne cocked his head as he studied her. "I'm sorry, but you just don't strike me as an agent. I mean…where's the training? If you're some secret agent, then how come you ran to Brodie for help? Why not take out the stalker yourself?"

Because she'd never taken anyone's life.

"I don't trust you," he said flatly. "I think you've been lying to the McGuires all along. You know more about their parents' death than you're saying. You know more about Stephen Brushard, and you're not getting out of here until I know every single one of your secrets."

BRODIE PACED BACK and forth in the narrow room. "This is ridiculous!" He glared at the two-way mirror to his right. "Why are we still in interrogation?"

Grant rolled his shoulders. "Probably because a man was shot to death right in front of us, and our plan to nab a killer resulted in a four-block radius of Austin being shut down for hours."

Brodie glared at his brother. "We answered their questions." Shayne had been the one to ask those questions, again and again. Shayne, the guy who was supposed to be his friend. The only cop who'd never given up the hunt for the people who'd killed Brodie's parents. *Now he's treating us all like suspects?*

"I'm sure we'll be given the all clear to go soon." Grant was probably trying to sound reassuring.

Brodie wasn't in the mood to be reassured. "Brushard's out there. You know he'll just come after her again. He'll keep coming until he gets her." Tension coiled within him. "And I'm tired of waiting for the guy to strike. I'm going after him. He'll see what it's like to be in the sights of a killer."

Grant shook his head. "You aren't a killer, Brodie."

"You shouldn't be so sure about that." Grant always saw just what he wanted to see... Sometimes, Brodie didn't think Grant realized who he had become.

"There are some lines that we can never cross, no matter how badly we may want to." Grant rose to his feet. Faced Brodie. "Your emotions can make you too dangerous—especially the emotions you feel for that woman."

"Jennifer," Brodie snapped. "Her name is—"

"How do you even know what her real name is? My contacts at the CIA turned up nothing on her."

"Because she had deep cover. She did. Nate did and—"

"Before he was shot, that Nate guy tried to kill Sullivan *and* Shayne. Not exactly the work of an upstanding government agent." Grant crossed his arms over his chest as he studied Brodie. "Are you certain you're making the right choice with her? Because, man, I'm not so sure you're thinking with a cool head on this one." A pause. "I'm not so sure you're using your head at all."

His brother was going to throw that bull at him? Grant sure wasn't in a position to judge. The guy had gone near crazy when the woman he loved—Scarlett Stone—had been threatened a few months back…and Scarlett had possessed plenty of secrets, too. "Grant—" Brodie began angrily.

The interrogation room door opened. A weary-looking Shayne stood on the threshold. "You two can go."

"About damn time," Brodie snapped.

Shayne's lips thinned. "A man died on my watch today. Because I agreed to help *you*." Shayne's expression was unyielding. "From here on out, I'm going by the book. And if the McGuires can't follow the law, you'll find yourselves under arrest."

Shayne was threatening them?

"Where's Jennifer?" Brodie asked as he strode toward Shayne. "I want her to—"

"She's not clear to leave."

"What?" He couldn't have just heard right.

"I'm holding her as a material witness."

No way. No—

"Don't worry, I'll put her in a safe house. She'll have around-the-clock guards."

"It's not her!" Brodie was less than a foot away from his friend. "It's Brushard. He's the one we need to take down!"

Shayne nodded. "And the Austin PD will take him down. The right way—I told you that before. We'll handle the case in a way that doesn't involve a shoot-out in the middle of the damn street." He gave Brodie a curt nod. "Now, you two are free to leave, but Ms. Wesley will be staying with me."

No way. "I want to see her."

Shayne hesitated. "That's not a good idea right now. She's in processing—"

"She didn't do anything wrong!"

"How do you know?" Shayne erupted. "I can't find a single detail about her from my government contacts. Nothing about her and nothing about the guy down in my morgue. I'm not going to let that woman slip through my fingers." His breath huffed out. "I became a target tonight. Nate Wesley tried to kill me. He was choking me when my car slammed into that pole. He was going to kill *me*."

"Shayne…"

"Cut your ties with Jennifer Wesley. She's not your problem any longer. She's mine."

The hell she was.

Shayne pointed at Brodie. At Grant. "I know you two think you're above the law, but you're not, and my friendship…it only extends so far. We've reached that line. Try to go over my head, try to interfere in my investigation, and I will lock you both up for obstruction."

The threat hung in the air for a moment; then Shayne turned and marched away. He didn't look back.

"What is happening here?" Brodie demanded.

Grant was staring after Shayne's retreating form.

"He can't just *keep* her…" Brodie needed to see Jennifer. He had to talk to her.

"Yes," Grant said softly, "he can."

We'll see about that.

WHEN THE DOOR to the interrogation room flew open, Jennifer's head snapped up. Her breath heaved from her as she stared—

At Brodie?

Jennifer jumped to her feet even as he hurried toward her.

"Sullivan!" she said instantly. "Is he—"

"He's fine. It's takes one hell of a lot more than that to take out my kid brother." He pulled her into his arms, held her tight. And it seemed as if Jennifer could *finally* draw in a deep breath.

His arms were so warm and strong around her, and Jennifer hadn't even realized how cold she'd been, not until that moment. "I understand," she told him. She needed to say those words. She looked up but didn't let him go. "I know why you're pulling away from me, and that's—"

He kissed her. Brodie's mouth crushed down on

her. There was nothing soft or gentle about that kiss. It was hard, consuming, burning with desire.

And maybe someone was watching them through that two-way mirror. Maybe it was a whole roomful of cops.

She didn't care. Her mouth opened beneath his, and Jennifer kissed him back as passionately as she could.

These may be my last moments with him. Part of her was very, very afraid that Brodie was just there to tell her goodbye.

Her lips parted even more. Her body was smashed into his, so tightly, so perfectly, and the fear was gone. With Brodie, need and desire were always so close to her surface. When he touched her, she let go of her control. She let go of her doubts.

She held on to him.

His tongue slid against hers. He growled low in his throat, and the kiss grew even more demanding. He was tasting her, taking her, and the kiss felt more like a claiming than anything else.

It didn't feel like goodbye.

More like a promise of passion to come.

His head slowly lifted, but his arms were still around her. She could feel his desire pressing into her.

"Brodie?" Jennifer shook her head, truly not understanding now. "You were watching the interrogation. You thought—"

"The hell I was." His words were an angry snarl. "Shayne had me and Grant in interrogation, too. Asking his questions again and again until I wanted to forget the fact that he was a friend and drive my fist into him."

Confused now, Jennifer shook her head again. "But…he said you were watching my interrogation. That you were angry with me because of what happened to Sullivan." She had a flash of Sullivan, pinned in that backseat. There had been blood all over his face—streaming down from what she knew had been a broken nose. She'd been so desperate to pull him out of that wreckage and to make sure that he was all right.

You have to be all right. Brodie needs you. You have to be all right. Only when Sullivan was finally clear of the car had Jennifer realized she'd been whispering those words again and again.

It was just that she knew how important Brodie's family was to him. A big part of her envied him that family connection. To be so tied to others, to know that they would *always* be there for you… She'd never had that.

She probably never would.

"He lied," Brodie said flatly. "Nate is the one that caused that wreck, and Brushard… I don't know how he knew to lie in wait at that exact spot, but he was ready for us. Almost like someone had tipped off the jerk."

She tried to remember more information about Stephen. "He had a network that he used. Blackmail was his specialty. He'd find people's weak points, and he'd use them. He'd get others to do his dirty work for him—that was why it was so hard to tie him to the crimes." Until she'd gotten lucky that night.

"He used Nate," Brodie said as his gaze sharpened on her. "And he's using someone else, too. Maybe someone in the police department. Shayne called the station before we left McGuire Securities—he told them we were coming in."

And then someone from the PD had contacted Stephen?

"He wants to put you in protective custody," Brodie said.

"What?"

"He says you're a material witness."

Her heart slammed into her chest. "I don't want to stay here." Because if someone was working with Stephen, she could be a sitting duck.

His forehead leaned down to touch hers. "I was afraid."

His confession seemed so stark in that narrow interrogation room.

"I looked down on the street, and you were a perfect target to him. I tried to warn you, but I was afraid it was too late." He kissed her again. A slow, long kiss. "I didn't want to lose you," he whispered.

Grant had been there, grabbing her, yanking her to safety.

"I want you in my life," Brodie told her. "When that SOB is locked up, when you're not always looking over your shoulder, I want you to stay with me."

Jennifer didn't know what to say.

"I want to know Jennifer Wesley and Jenny Belmont. Hell, I want to know you—*under any name you want*. In that moment, when I was so damn afraid you'd die before me, I knew...Jennifer, I knew that what I feel for you isn't just some desire that's going to wane. I've wanted you for years, and now that you're back in my life—"

The door opened behind them. "Brodie?" Shayne demanded, voice sharp with surprise. "What the hell are you doing in here? There was supposed to be a guard on this room!"

"I'm not going to just watch you leave again," Brodie finished softly. Then he kissed her once more, not seeming to care that the detective was marching toward them.

"Brodie!"

Taking his time, Brodie lifted his head.

Shayne grabbed his shoulder and pulled him back. "You can't be in here."

Brodie just shrugged, not looking particularly concerned.

"She's in police custody now. This isn't a PI case anymore."

Jennifer twisted her hands in front of her.

"Nate Wesley is on a slab in my morgue. But according to every file I can find, that guy died in a boating accident. So now I have to deal with a man who'd died—twice—and I have to stop some criminal who broke out of a Russian jail and is determined to bring hell to *my* town." Shayne huffed out a breath. "So I'm telling you…the McGuires have to back off on this one. I've taken over, and I'll protect her. Trust me."

"When it comes to Jennifer," Brodie said with a slow roll of his shoulders that somehow appeared menacing, "I don't trust many people." His eyes were filled with a turbulent green fire. "And I think you've got a leak in the PD. Someone tipped off Brushard—that's how he knew where to wait for us. Someone here—"

"You think I don't know that?" Shayne demanded quietly as his gaze cut toward the two-way mirror. "*I'm* the one who'll be taking her into custody. I'm the one who'll stay with her. You can count on me to protect her."

Brodie shook his head.

Shayne straightened his shoulders. As Jennifer watched, his expression became cold. Hard. This was the cop she was staring at, not Brodie's friend, not any longer. "This isn't up for debate. That woman is a material witness, and she's stay-

ing in police custody. Fight me on this, and I'll lock
you up."

Brodie's hands had fisted. "Be very careful," he
murmured, "about starting a war with me."

"I don't have a choice." Shayne marched back
toward the interrogation door. He yanked it open
and called for officers. Three uniformed men hurried inside. Shayne inclined his head toward Brodie. "Escort Mr. McGuire outside. Make absolutely
certain that he leaves the station. If he doesn't, if he
fights you, put him in lockup."

Brodie took a menacing step forward. Jennifer
grabbed his arm. "Don't."

His enraged stare met hers.

"Don't do it. If you get locked up, that's not going
to help anyone." She tried to smile for him, but it
was hard when she just wanted to grab him and hold
on tight. "I'll be okay."

"Escort him *out*," Shayne ordered. "And make
sure he doesn't bribe his way back inside."

"I'll be okay," Jennifer said again as those cops
closed in on him.

His gaze raked over her face. "Remember what I
said. I won't just watch you leave. *Trust me.*"

The cops pulled him toward the door.

You don't have to watch me leave this time,
Jennifer thought. *I'm watching you.*

The door shut behind him.

"THANKS ONE HELL of a lot," Brodie snarled as the uniforms left him outside the PD. They flushed and muttered apologies.

"Uh…getting kicked out of a police station?" Grant asked, striding toward him as he shook his head. "That's a new one, even for you."

He whirled on his brother. "Shayne's trying to take her away."

"In light of what happened, you don't think that might be a good thing? Until Brushard is caught—"

"How would you feel if someone took Scarlett from you?" Scarlett was the woman that Grant had loved for most of his life. Loved—and nearly lost far too recently. Now Grant guarded the woman like a hawk.

Grant's jaw hardened. "You know what that would be like for me."

"Then don't tell me this is a good thing. I need to be close to her." He glared up at the police station. Shayne wasn't going to shut him out. Not when Jennifer's safety was on the line.

"What can I do?" Grant asked him.

And that was the way things were with them. Always had been. "Sullivan needs you now." Their brother was in the hospital, and he needed family close to him. "Davis and I…we can handle this." Davis had connections that he could use. Connections he *would* use.

"How close are you about to get to breaking the law?"

He tilted back his head as he stared at the PD once more. "It's about to get bent."

"I DON'T UNDERSTAND… Why are you doing this?" Jennifer turned to face Detective Shayne Townsend. They'd just entered the "safe house," but Jennifer was sure not feeling safe as she stood there with him.

The little apartment was on a back street in Austin, positioned up on the third floor of a run-down building. The elevator had been broken, so they'd climbed the three flights of stairs that took them up to the apartment.

The carpet was threadbare beneath her feet. The only furniture in the small den was a sagging sofa and a small wooden coffee table.

"I'm trying to keep you alive, Ms. Wesley." He double-checked the locks. Another cop was outside. Shayne had given him orders to check the perimeter.

"I was alive with Brodie."

"You jeopardized his family. In case you didn't notice, nothing comes before family. Not for the McGuires."

She rubbed her chilled arms. "You said that Sullivan was all right."

"He is…but if there are too many more run-ins with your stalker, I might not be able to say that for long." He motioned toward the door on the right. "There's a bedroom in there for you to use. We've only got one bathroom in this joint, so we'll be sharing."

Right. She glanced down at the floor.

"We got the results back on that knife that Brodie found at the Montgomery ranch."

Her gaze whipped back up to him.

"No prints. The only DNA was yours. Your blood."

Stephen had been very careful. "So we're back to nothing."

He shook his head. "We're back to looking for a ghost." He opened his briefcase and pulled out a file. She inched closer to him so that she could see the name on that file. "Stephen Brushard."

She stared at the name, and, suddenly, she wasn't in a run-down apartment. She was back in Russia. In a ballroom, in a castle. A place right out of a dream. And Stephen had been there. Bowing to her. Asking her to dance.

For a moment, she'd forgotten that she was just living a lie. She'd thought she was living a dream.

Prince Charming.

Then she'd found out that he was the real villain of the tale.

"He's dead." Shayne pulled out a typewritten report. One written in Russian. "He was attacked in his cell."

She grabbed the report. Scanned it. Stephen had been found with a knife in his side. He'd been alive when he went to the infirmary, but he hadn't survived long after that. His body had been cremated within hours of his death. That recorded death had happened a year ago.

"Not him," Jennifer said flatly. "He didn't die—he just escaped." But at least they had a timeline now. So Stephen couldn't have killed Brodie's parents. But…maybe someone he'd hired had? The same person who'd taken that picture of her at the ranch.

"You can read Russian?"

She almost rolled her eyes. "I was a spy. Do you think they would have sent me out to all of those countries if I only spoke English?" She'd had a gift for language and an ability to drop and acquire an accent at will.

His eyes narrowed.

She tapped the file. "Nate got a death certificate, too. It was as fake as Stephen's."

But the cop didn't look convinced. "Maybe he *did* die in that prison and we're looking for someone in Stephen's family…someone who wants to get some payback against you."

She scanned the file he had. She had to give the cop credit; he'd definitely been digging in the right places. There were multiple reports of injuries, of attacks, on Stephen. He'd been in and out of the prison infirmary almost every week.

I'm going to torture you...

There was a photo in the file. A grainy image of Stephen Brushard, one that must have been taken shortly after his incarceration. His thick black hair was smoothed back from his forehead. His square jaw was clenched, and, even in the picture, she could see the fury in his eyes.

Stephen had been a handsome man, debonair, charming. But beneath that facade, he'd been rotten to the core.

"Just look at the McGuires," Shayne said quietly. "Sometimes, families want blood for blood."

She pushed the file back at him. "The McGuires aren't planning to kill anyone." She spun away from him. Paced toward the lone window in the room.

He laughed, and the sound held no humor. "Aren't they? I guess you don't know Brodie nearly as well as you think."

The window was covered with a layer of brown grime so thick she could barely see outside.

"They're going to destroy every person involved in their parents' deaths. It's just a matter of time."

There was something in his voice...almost resignation. Bitterness.

She glanced back at him.

His eyes—flint hard—were on her. "Brodie was

helping you only because you were a way to get to Stephen Brushard. You were expendable to him."

He was wrong. "You don't know what you're talking about." There was so much more between her and Brodie. When he held her…she was safe. She could trust him with all her secrets.

With him, there was no longer a need for lies.

"I got you away from Brodie. I did it for your protection. You can't count on him. But you can count on me."

Could she? Jennifer wasn't about to give her trust to him. *I trust Brodie.*

"I can help you."

Her instincts were screaming at her again. Something was just…off with him. "How long have you been friends with Brodie?"

"We went to school together. Grew up together. I've always known the McGuires." He didn't move from his position. A stance that put him right between Jennifer and the apartment's door. Its only exit. "That's why I never gave up on his parents' case. I figured I owed them."

He shifted his stance a bit, and her gaze dipped to the gun holstered just beneath his left arm.

"Brodie and the others didn't give up, either. They kept searching. Kept pushing until they found the murder weapons used for the crime."

Jennifer tried to keep her body relaxed, her hands

loose at her sides. And she refused to let any expression show on her face.

"They found the guns…and then they found you."

Something is wrong. The whole scene felt off for her. He'd separated her from Brodie, taken her away from the police station. Stashed her in this apartment…

"You gave his parents fifty thousand dollars."

"Did Brodie tell you that?" She deliberately let her words tremble a bit, wanting to look weak right then. If she looked weak, then maybe he wouldn't see the threat coming from her, not until it was too late.

He inclined his head. "Why did you give them the money?"

The answer was simple enough. "Because Brodie saved my life."

He stalked across the room. She tensed, and, once more, her gaze fell to his gun.

Why didn't he keep me at the station?

And where was the other cop? The one who'd ridden over with them? Just how long did it take to do a perimeter search?

"Why did they want the money?"

"I don't know!"

He grabbed her arms. Shook her. "Liar!"

What? They had just stepped right over into bad cop land.

"You expect me to believe you gave two strangers fifty thousand dollars?"

"They weren't strangers. They were Brodie's parents."

He shoved her back. Her shoulders hit the window. "Stop it!" Jennifer yelled at him.

But lines of fury were stamped onto his face. "I won't let you ruin everything for me."

What in the hell? And suddenly Jennifer was very afraid that she'd found the cop who had tipped off Stephen before.

"You can't ruin it, not when I worked so hard to get my life back on track. I just... I can't let you destroy it all."

His hands were hard around her shoulders.

"Maybe it would be better if you just disappeared," he fired. "Easier for everyone."

Was he threatening her? Because the chill that had just went down her spine sure said he was.

And if this guy was the one who'd sold her out to Stephen before... *Then he's done it again now.*

THE YOUNG COP was ridiculously obvious.

Just because he'd put on some old torn jeans and a T-shirt, did the kid really think that made him look like he fit in with the neighborhood?

The guy looked as if he was barely twenty-one, and his nervous gaze kept sweeping the scene as he glanced to the left, then the right.

Too easy.

He sauntered toward the run-down building. He'd watched Jennifer go in there less than fifteen minutes before. Time for him to go claim his prize.

"Hey, kid," he muttered to the boy.

The cop whirled toward him.

He drove his knife right into the boy's stomach, held the blade there as the cop's eyes widened in horror.

"Which floor?"

The cop grunted.

"Want me to twist the knife?"

"Th-third…"

Smiling, he twisted the knife anyway. Because he could.

Because he'd never really liked cops anyway.

Chapter Ten

"Brodie, are you sure this is a good idea?" Davis asked as their car pulled to a stop. "She's in protective custody. The cops have her. The woman is safe."

If she was safe, then why were his guts in knots?

"How did you even find this damn place?" Davis wanted to know.

"I bribed the right people at the police station." It wasn't like Shayne was his only friend there.

Davis swore. "Then let's just hope that Stephen Brushard doesn't know those same people or your lady is going to be in serious trouble." Davis had been brought up to speed—*fast*—on Brushard. And when he'd met Brodie, the guy had come bearing a gift—a report on Stephen Brushard that Mac had been able to dig up using his contacts.

Thanks to that report, they now had a face to go with the SOB's name. Stephen Brushard had grown up the only child of a wealthy New York family. He'd gone to all the right schools, knew all the right people…

On the surface, he'd seemed like a legitimate businessman.

But Jennifer had found out the truth about him.

Brodie took one more look down at Brushard's picture. Black hair, blue eyes, cleft in his chin. He had the stats on the guy, too. Six foot three, two hundred pounds. Or at least, that had been his weight before he'd spent those years in prison.

Prison could change a man, on the inside and outside.

Brodie shut off his penlight and stared up at the apartment building. "What's the plan now?" Davis wanted to know. "You run in, guns blazing?"

"No." More finesse would be needed until he could figure out just what game Shayne thought he was playing. *Why did you take her? Why keep me from her?* "You watch the front, and I'll go up the fire escape." That fire escape would take him all the way up to the third floor. Shayne had tried to keep the location secret, but the guy obviously didn't realize that half of his department owed favors to the McGuires. Brodie had called in some of those favors.

"Right. So you want me to just stay here…"

He pulled his gun from the glove box. "And if you see Stephen Brushard, you stop him. With any force necessary." He shoved open his door, but Davis caught his shoulder.

"And if you see him," Davis told him. "Don't you hesitate—got it? Protect yourself. Protect Jennifer."

He would.

Brodie slipped from the vehicle. Not his car because he hadn't wanted anyone to follow him back to Jennifer. He'd made sure that no one was behind him and Davis when they headed to this street.

Music and laughter drifted from a nearby bar. Since it was closing in on 4:00 a.m., the late-night crowd was packing it in, and voices floated to him. He swept around the side of the building, his gaze drifting up to the third floor. Lights were on up there, and those lights were like a beacon to him.

I'm coming, Jennifer.

He grabbed for the fire-escape ladder, but then...

Then he spotted a dark liquid on the ground to the right. It gleamed under the old street light. A pool of water? What the hell?

He bent, frowning, as he looked at that pool.

Brodie realized he wasn't staring at water...just as he heard a faint groan.

Not water. *Blood.*

The groan came again, the sound so close, seeming to originate from right behind a pile of garbage. He hurried toward that garbage, his gun out. "I'm armed," he said. "So you'd better—"

There was more blood. Far too much.

He shoved away the garbage and saw the crumpled form—a man, young, clean-shaven—who'd been tossed away.

Left to die.

Brodie jerked out his phone. Called 9-1-1 and—

"What is the nature of your emergency?"

The man groaned once more, a low, weak sound. With that much blood loss, how was he even alive? "Help…" the guy whispered, "her…"

Brodie spun back around and stared up at the third floor. Only the lights had just flashed off. The whole building was in total darkness.

"WHAT THE HELL?" Shayne demanded as he pulled his hands away from her.

They were surrounded by darkness. Her heart slammed into her chest because Jennifer knew. *This isn't good.*

The only light in the place came from the window—faint streetlight that managed to peek through the layer of brown grime.

"He found me," Jennifer whispered.

"The building's old," Shayne said. "A fuse could have blown. *Anything* could have happened."

She heard the floor creak beneath his feet. "The door's locked," he said a few moments later. "This place is secure. I'll call Randy and get him to tell us what's happening."

"Randy?"

"The cop on patrol outside."

When he pulled out his phone, the illumination lit up the hard lines of his face.

She caught her breath while she waited for him to make a connection with Randy. She wanted that other cop to pick up, to tell them everything was fine and—

"Randy?" Shayne demanded. "What's going on out there? We just went dark."

She exhaled slowly. Randy was okay. He was still patrolling.

"What? I can hardly hear you."

Jennifer turned and curled her fingers around the window. She shoved, trying to lift it up, but it was stuck. So she shoved even harder.

Nothing.

"Where are you? Yeah, yeah, I'll let you in." He ended the call, but he must have still been using his flashlight app because he shone that light right on her as he pointed his phone in her direction. "Randy's on the stairs. He said the whole building went dark."

"Stephen is here. You know he is."

The light swung away from her and hit the front door. She grabbed for the window and yanked harder. It lifted—about one inch.

"It could be coincidence—"

Her laughter cut him off. "Come on. You're a cop! You know better. It's him. He followed you or he made someone at the PD tell him where we were."

Did you tell him, Detective Townsend? Her breath came out in heaving pants. "And I can't help but wonder, did you want him to find me? Are *you* the one who tipped him off?"

Silence.

"Because I don't understand what's been happening since you had me in that interrogation room! Something is going on and I just—"

"The money was for me."

That little reveal had her tensing…and her hands shoved harder against the window. It slid up a few more inches. Not enough for her to slip out, not yet.

Is the fire escape on the other side of the window? It had better be. Or else her escape plan wasn't going to work at all.

"I was in trouble. In deep…and if I didn't pay up, then my life would have been over."

"What are you talking about?" she whispered.

"They weren't supposed to get hurt. No one was."

Her shoulders hunched back.

"But maybe…hell, maybe they were watching me the whole time. Maybe they thought the Mc-Guires had more money, and that's why they went back to them."

A hard pounding shook the front door.

"I'll lose it all if the truth comes out," Shayne said, his voice thick.

"I don't understand what's happening!"

"I shot a man. I was young then, inexperienced…

It was a mistake. But they knew. They saw me. Saw the cover-up."

And, just like that, she did understand. "Blackmail."

"Hurry, Townsend," a voice called out from the other side of the front door. "Let me in!"

"I paid, and that should have been the end." His voice was still low, but she heard him clearly. His light was on the door, but he wasn't opening it. "But it's never the end. Once they've got you on the hook, you are theirs for life."

Her gaze was on the door, the only thing she could see in that room. "Randy… That's not Randy out there, is it?"

"He told me that he'd keep it all quiet, if I just let him have you."

"He's lying," she whispered. "Please, don't open that front door."

"He has the video of the shooting. The kid wasn't armed! I—I thought he was." A beat of silence then, "I don't know how Brushard got it, but he'll air it, and I'll lose everything."

That was the way Stephen had worked before. Find a weak spot and exploit it. It was obvious that Stephen knew the detective's weakness.

The door shook.

"Brodie thinks I've been his friend. And I am… *I am.*"

But he was walking toward the door.

Jennifer spun around and crawled through the window. She grabbed for the fire escape, but—a hand grabbed *her*.

She screamed.

And that hand jerked her out of the room. Right into—

"I've got you." Brodie's voice.

She'd been jerked into Brodie's arms.

He'd been there? Standing out on that fire escape? Had he heard Shayne's confession?

"Go down the fire escape," he ordered. "Davis is down there. More cops are coming. *Go.*"

She rushed down the old steps, and the fire escape shook beneath her. Her hands flew over the railing. Down, down she went; then Jennifer jumped the last few feet to the ground below.

And she saw the body.

Just thrown away, like garbage. She hurried to the man's side. "Randy?"

Her hand went to his throat. She couldn't find a pulse.

Shots rang out from above, and when she looked up, she saw the flash of the gunfire, like lightning flickering from within that third-floor apartment.

Fear stole her breath. *Brodie.*

"What are you doing?" Brodie demanded as he shoved Shayne against the wall. "You're firing your weapon straight at the door! Someone could be—"

"He's on the other side. The man who wants to hurt your precious Jennifer. The man who wants to kill her." Shayne laughed. "Maybe I should have let him. Maybe everything would have been easier then."

Brodie yanked the gun away from Shayne. "*You're a cop!* Act like one." The guy had been feeding him that bull about doing things the *right* way, and now this—

"I did it," Shayne whispered. "I'm the one. They were helping me!"

Brodie battled back his fury and his growing fear. "Look, I don't have time for this garbage right now. Randy is dead, and that jerk Stephen is—"

"He was on the other side of the door. I shot him! Chose to kill him, not her."

Brodie backed away from him because Shayne wasn't making any sense. Carefully, he opened the front door.

It was pitch-black out there. Carefully, he inched out into that hallway. Even in the darkness, it only took a few seconds to realize—

You didn't shoot anyone, Shayne.

Because Brodie didn't find anyone in that hallway.

"RANDY? RANDY, PLEASE!" She didn't want more blood on her hands. She didn't want this cop to die. She—

Felt a gun press into the back of her head.

"It was taking too long for the dirty cop to answer the door. So I thought it might be better to step outside."

Once again, that voice was familiar, but this time, she knew exactly who was talking to her—knew who held that gun to her head. Stephen.

She froze.

"We're going to leave now, Jennifer. Just you and me. We're going to walk away, and if you come quietly, no one else has to die."

He pulled Jennifer to her feet.

"You don't want anyone else to die, do you?"

Her eyes were on the shadowy, still form of the young cop.

"You don't want your lover to die. You don't want his brothers to die. Hell, I bet you even would like for me to spare the life of the cop who sold you out."

"I never wanted anyone to die." Very, very slowly she turned to face Stephen. "Not even you."

He laughed, and the sound was cold and chilling. "That's right. You just wanted me to rot in prison, didn't you?"

Sirens screamed in the distance.

"It's time for us to go," Stephen said. His arm wrapped around her. He pulled her close, his left arm slung around her shoulders and the gun now pressed to her side as they walked away from the apartment building. To any onlookers, they probably resembled a couple. Lovers.

He put his mouth close to her ear. "If you call for help, I will shoot anyone who is dumb enough to rush to your rescue."

They'd left the alley. They were heading down the block.

"Jennifer?"

She swallowed. A man was running toward them. The streetlight fell over his face. Not Brodie...

Brodie's face, but that was Davis's voice.

She could already feel Stephen reacting. At her name, he'd jerked, and he'd yanked the weapon up to aim it at Davis.

Davis can't die! Brodie needs him!

She surged forward even as she grabbed for the gun. She tried to put herself in the path of that weapon so the shot wouldn't hit—

It hit her. The bullet slammed into her side, and the pain burned through her.

"Jennifer!" Davis's frantic shout.

But Stephen had dragged her up against him once more. And Davis— Davis had dodged for cover. Good...good...he was safe.

Her fingers went to her side. Pressed down. Blood spilled over her hand.

"Bad mistake, Jennifer, so very bad," Stephen whispered. "You know I don't plan to let you die easily."

No, he had other plans, but at least Davis was safe.

Stephen began hauling her to the right, toward the street. A sedan waited there. *His car?*

"Let her go!" Davis ordered.

Stephen laughed. "Just like your brother, hmm? And where is that brother of yours? Dying upstairs, while you waste your time trying to protect her down here?"

Her body trembled. "Go…back up… Brodie!"

"Your brother trusted the wrong man. You all did. I saw the photos. I watched the video. I know what Detective Townsend did… A killer, and you thought *he* was helping you to find your parents' murderer? He was just steering you the wrong way all along."

They were at the sedan. The gun was still pressed tightly to her and his hold on her was unbreakable.

"I can't let you take her," Davis yelled. He'd abandoned his cover, and Jennifer saw that he'd drawn his weapon, a weapon aimed at her and Stephen.

"What will you do then? Shoot? If you do, you'll hit her, and she's already nearly bleeding out. Will you kill the woman that your brother loves?"

"He…doesn't…" Jennifer managed to say. She was trembling harder now.

"I don't think you will." Stephen was so confident. So cocky. "I think you're going to lower your gun right now…and back the hell up."

"N-no," Jennifer whispered. "If…you…he'll sh-shoot…"

But Davis was hesitating. He started to lower his weapon. *No!*

Only instead of shooting at Davis then—as she'd feared, Stephen shoved Jennifer into the car. He jumped in behind her even as Davis fired off a round at them.

Then Stephen had the car rumbling to life. He slammed down on the gas pedal as Jennifer tried frantically to open the passenger-side door. But her fingers were slick with blood, and she couldn't get the lock to disengage.

Stephen spun the car around.

She hit the side of the door, and her wound burned even more. Then she realized *why* he'd spun that car around.

He was heading straight for Davis. Davis was in the road, yelling for her, and Stephen was going to run him down.

She grabbed for the wheel. Stephen shoved her away.

Davis leaped to the side of the street, but Stephen just jerked the wheel. Davis wasn't firing his weapon. He must have been still afraid of hitting her. The headlights from Stephen's car were shining right on him as the car raced forward.

At the last moment, Davis jumped into the alleyway.

Stephen's car slammed into a garbage can. Stephen lost control of the wheel a moment as the vehicle careened across the street. Then, with a curse, Stephen shot his car forward.

Her fingers were still fumbling with the lock.

"You can give that up," he muttered. "I knew you'd be going for a ride with me. The lock is broken." He glanced her way. "From here on out, it's just going to be me and you."

"No, no, no!"

Brodie burst out of the building just as he heard his brother's furious shout.

"Davis!"

His brother was in the middle of the street. At Brodie's shout, Davis swung toward him. "He took her!"

Brodie shook his head.

"Come on! We can catch them!" Davis jumped into the car they'd used before. Revved the engine.

Sirens were closing in. Screaming. So loud now.

And Jennifer was…gone?

Brodie dived into the car. He'd barely gotten inside when Davis slammed his foot down on the gas pedal. The car fishtailed and screeched down the street.

"We're looking for a dark sedan," Davis gritted out. "Late model. No license plate. And…you need to know, he…he shot her."

The blood seemed to freeze in Brodie's veins.

"He was going to shoot me," Davis continued as they raced down the road. "But she jumped in his way. She took that bullet. I'm so damn sorry."

"There!" Brodie yelled because he'd just caught sight of the car. At least, he thought that was the car. Driving hell fast, no license plate on the back. *I'm coming, Jennifer.*

"He said…he said you were getting shot—that Shayne was turning on you."

Brodie couldn't think of Shayne's betrayal right then. "Go faster!" He'd left his old friend behind because he'd been so worried about Jennifer.

The sedan screeched around a corner.

Davis surged after them, but a taxi turned right in front of them. Davis yelled and jerked the wheel hard, narrowly avoiding that taxi. Then he pounded on the horn. "Get out of the way!" Davis shouted.

The driver shouted back and slowly moved. Moved *too* slowly. Because by the time they rounded that corner, there was no sign of the sedan.

The road to the left was empty.

The road to the right was littered with a few cars—only none of them were sedans.

"Which way?" Davis demanded.

Brodie stared down those roads. "Right." Because it would have been easier for the jerk to blend and vanish in that bit of traffic. "They went right."

Davis spun the wheel, and they gave chase again.

STEPHEN DRAGGED HER out of the car. He'd taken her into an old garage, one a few yards off the road. She could hear the buzz of traffic around her.

"They're not going to find you. They'll just drive past us." His hand locked around her side, right over the bullet wound. "By the time anyone finds you, it will be too late."

He yanked her forward, and she realized he'd been staying there—in that abandoned garage. Because there were supplies inside. Glowing lanterns. Rope. Handcuffs. Knives.

This is where he'll kill me.

He pushed her into a chair, tied her legs to the wood. Yanked her arms behind her back and handcuffed her so tightly that she had to choke back a cry of pain.

Then he crouched before her, putting his face right in front of hers. It was her first time seeing him clearly, and Jennifer gasped.

This wasn't the man she remembered. Gone was the handsome, suave businessman who'd lied so easily as he destroyed lives.

His face was haggard, his eyes wild. His hair had been shaved, a buzz cut that made him look even deadlier.

And...there were scars on his face. A slash on his cheekbone. A long, thick line on his throat. His nose had been broken—by the looks of things, at least a few times.

"Kill or be killed... That was the law where you sent me."

"I was doing my job! You were selling drugs, weapons!"

"The Russian mob thought I'd betrayed them. They couldn't figure out how the authorities had gotten all that intel. They didn't know about you."

He put the gun on the floor.

"I knew about you, though. I put the pieces together. There were a few people—so damn few—who were still loyal to me." He caught her chin in his hand to force her to keep staring into his eyes. "I got one of those men to keep watch on you. He was my eyes, when I couldn't be there to see you for myself. He followed you, noticed the pattern. Wherever you and your dear old dad went, arrests seemed to follow you."

"Stop blaming me!" she yelled at him. "*You* were the one selling the weapons. You were the one making the drugs. You were—"

His fingers dug into her skin. "If I'd never met you, I wouldn't have gone to hell. Because that's what that Russian prison was...hell. Every day was a battle. The attacks never stopped. At one point, I even wanted to die." He smiled. "Then I realized... I couldn't. Not yet. Because somewhere, you were out there. And you had to pay for what you'd done to me."

He freed her. Rose to his feet. Stalked away.

She twisted her wrists, struggling against the cuffs.

"Once I got out, it was easy enough to track you down. Getting out—that took some time."

"You faked your death."

He laughed, the sound rough. "Guess that was something Nate and I had in common."

Nate. The pain in her heart was worse than the throbbing burn of her bullet wound. "You went after Nate. You killed his wife!"

Stephen glanced back at her, surprise rippling over his face. "Is that what he told you? Oh, I see… He probably spun some bull about me killing the old broad because that made it look like he *had* to turn on you." He laughed again, the sound seeming to echo around them. "That woman is dead, all right, but not by my hand. Nate got bored. He got tired of living an *ordinary* life."

Jennifer shook her head. "No, you're—"

"I planned to kill him. I mean, he was helping you back in Russia, wasn't he? But I thought I'd use him first. So I just offered him money. Money to help me get to you. Told him that when you were cold in the ground, he'd get a big payday."

Her wrists twisted inside the cuffs.

"He'd gone from living like a billionaire to living

on a clipping-coupons budget. He *jumped* at the chance to turn on you."

She swallowed. "I don't believe you."

"I don't care." He turned his back. Kept walking. "Cling to your delusions if that makes you feel better. If you'd rather he turned on you because he was facing his own death—go right ahead." He stopped near a table and picked up a gleaming knife. "But the truth is this… He didn't care about you. No one has ever cared. You're disposable. To the government. To Nate."

Each word seemed to stab into her.

"You wrecked lives, and now, it's your turn to suffer."

The hell it was.

He advanced on her.

"I saved lives!" Jennifer shouted at him as she lifted her chin. "Innocent lives. Women and children in France. Refugees in the Middle East. Orphans in Russia. Yeah—the same orphans you were trying to use as drug mules." Her breath rushed out. "I put away criminals. Men like you who deserved to be behind bars. So spin me your lies about how I messed up your life, if that's what *you* have to believe, but the truth is…" Her chest heaved. "The truth is that you destroyed yourself long before I ever came along."

He held her stare a moment longer. Then he glanced down at the blade in his hand.

THE YOUNG COP was dead. Shayne Townsend gazed at Randy Mullins. The rookie had been so excited about his job. So eager to help.

"What happened here?"

Shayne looked over his shoulder and saw Grant McGuire pushing his way through the small crowd that had gathered on the street.

Grant saw him and shouted, "Shayne! Shayne, where is Brodie?"

Shayne turned away from the sight of that still cop. *His death is on me.* He hadn't intended for the man to get hurt. There were so many things he hadn't intended. He strode toward Grant. "I'm sorry."

Grant blanched. "No, not Brodie—"

"He's not here. Jennifer was taken, and Brodie went after her."

Grant spun away, but Shayne grabbed his shoulder before he could leave. "I…I haven't been…the friend you thought." Once, he and Grant had been so very close.

Once.

"Shayne?" Now there was suspicion in Grant's voice. On his face.

Shayne swallowed and said, "Call Brodie. Tell him…Fifteen-seventy-eight Ridgeway. That's where he'll find the man he's looking for." He flashed his friend a tired smile. "If I don't find him first."

Because he wasn't going to have Jennifer Wesley's blood on his hands. He wasn't going to hurt the McGuires again.

His career was over. The lies...the secrets...they were all about to come out into the open.

BRODIE'S PHONE RANG, vibrating in his pocket. He yanked it up, saw the name on the screen, then shoved the phone against his ear. "Grant, the guy has Jennifer! We lost them and I need you to—"

"Fifteen-seventy-eight Ridgeway."

"What?"

"Shayne said you needed to get there. He's on his way, too, and as soon as these cops get out of my way—" anger roughened Grant's voice "—I'll be en route."

"Turn the car around," Brodie snapped to Davis. *"Now."*

There were other voices on the line. He heard the cops questioning Grant.

"Fifteen-seventy-eight Ridgeway," Brodie told his brother as a cold chill pierced his heart.

They'd passed that street fifteen minutes ago. It would take them that long—maybe less—to get back.

So much could happen in a few moments' time.

In a few moments, a person could live...

Or a person could die.

Chapter Eleven

Jennifer screamed when the blade sliced down her arm.

"That was my first wound in prison. A guy knifed me because he didn't like the way I looked." Stephen leaned toward Jennifer. "Guess what I don't like about you?"

She clamped her lips together. He'd moved so fast with that first attack, lunging forward and driving that knife into her. She'd be prepared next time. Jennifer braced herself.

He smiled and lifted the knife.

"Your SEAL didn't realize we turned off the main road. He's probably still driving hell fast, so sure that he'll find you and save the day." He tapped the bloody knife beneath his chin. "What do you think he'll do when he finds your body? Will he break? I mean, the guy already walks on an edge, from what I've heard about him. He likes violence, the rush from adrenaline, the thrill of the hunt. Your death might just push him too far."

Jennifer shook her head. "Brodie isn't like that."

"Oh, really? You think you know him because you had sex with the guy?"

She did know him. She stared up at Stephen. "He's not evil. He's not like you."

He lunged toward her. The knife sliced down her shoulder. She didn't scream this time.

How much time has passed? The bullet wound still bled, her whole body shuddered and, when she glanced down, Jennifer saw that her blood had dripped onto the floor.

"How the mighty have fallen," he murmured. "No fancy ball gowns for you now. Just a cape of blood."

"I was…never one for fancy ball gowns anyway."

He lifted the knife.

"Why did Detective Townsend help you?"

Stephen's lips curled.

"Nate…you said he helped you for money. Why did Shayne do it? He…he's the one who told you I was at the safe house, right?" If she could keep him talking, then she might be able to think of some way to escape.

Or at least she'd buy herself a few more precious moments of life. Because she didn't know if he was still planning for a long, slow end for her. With Brodie hunting him, Stephen could snap at any moment. *And kill me.*

"I found the detective's weak spot." He sounded

pleased with himself. "Though, really, I guess I ow⟨
that to you."

Jennifer shook her head. "I don't understand."

"I told you already…I had a few people who wer⟨
still loyal to me. One was watching you. He'd tol⟨
me about your little—ah—incident in the Middl⟨
East."

She stiffened. "*You* did that." Now she understoo⟨
just how her cover had been blown on that case.

He inclined his head as if accepting a compli
ment. "My associate did. He let the right peopl⟨
know that you needed to be eliminated. Though h⟨
assured me you'd suffer before your end." His fac⟨
hardened. "*Then* you got away."

Thanks to Brodie.

"That associate followed you. It seemed s⟨
strange for a woman like you to rush all the way
back to a little ranch in Austin, Texas. When he tol⟨
me about your visit, I thought perhaps I'd foun⟨
your weak point. A family, nestled away all saf⟨
and sound."

"They weren't my family," she whispered. *Dea*⟨
God, is that why they died? Stephen had though⟨
they were her parents?

"He kept watching. Saw you make the cash dro⟨
to them…saw the cop." He laughed. "My guy go⟨
curious, so he hung around. He wanted to kno⟨
why that little ranch was getting so much action."

She stopped struggling in the chair. "You didn't kill the McGuires?"

"That one isn't on me. Haven't you realized yet? I like for my prey to suffer. You cross me, you pay. But the McGuires—"

"They were shot. Killed quickly."

Not by his hand.

"My associate got pictures of the cop. He saw him taking the money. Saw him use that cash with some rather unsavory characters."

Seriously? Like he could judge *unsavory*.

"I found out about the body Shayne Townsend wanted to keep buried. I used that. Told the guy I'd turn all those photos over to the media...to the Mc-Guires...if he didn't give me what I wanted."

So Shayne had traded his life for her own.

"That cop had gotten trigger-happy. Shot a kid that he thought had a weapon, but it turned out the kid wasn't armed. He hid that kill. Fool should have known the dead would come back to haunt him."

She heaved in the chair. Was the right chair leg loose? It felt that way. "Do the dead haunt you? Because they should."

The knife's blade pressed onto her cheek, but he didn't slice deep, not yet. Stephen's left hand rose and traced over the wound on *his* cheek. "I got this scar from a Ukrainian who wanted my food."

He was going to cut open her face. She shoved

back against the chair. It toppled, sending her crashing to the floor.

Stephen snarled and jumped toward her with his knife.

"Stop!" a voice thundered. "Stop or I will shoot you."

Stephen halted, that knife of his inches away from her. "The cop! *You're* the one who dared to come here?"

Her head turned. She could see Shayne, standing a few feet away, his weapon drawn.

Stephen rose, and his laughter echoed in the garage. "You're the one here to save the day? You're the killer. You don't get to play hero!"

"I'm not playing anything. Drop the knife. *Now.*"

Stephen dropped the knife. It clattered to the floor. "I have those photographs. They're in a very safe place, but that place won't stay safe…not if you don't get out of here!"

Shayne shook his head. "I won't let you kill her."

She heaved with her legs. The chair had shattered beneath her, and the ropes around her feet had loosened. Her hands were still handcuffed, but she was fighting fiercely to escape her bonds. "He has a gun, Shayne!"

"And I also have your life in my hands, Detective," Stephen ground out. "That wonderful life of yours…your accommodations, your reputation, your job…I can destroy it all."

Shayne took a step toward him. "I can't let you kill her."

"Why?" Stephen snarled back. "Because you're such an upstanding citizen? I *know* your secrets."

Shayne raised his gun. "Step away from her. Move back, now!"

Stephen retreated, a small movement. "You're making a mistake here, Detective. One that you will regret."

"No." Shayne gave a hard shake of his head. "I'm finally doing something right. I've got enough to regret in my life already. I won't add more." He bent near Jennifer. "It's going to be all right," he whispered to her. "I'll get you out of here."

A gunshot blasted. Shayne jerked against her.

"No," Stephen said softly as Shayne slumped beside Jennifer. "You won't."

BRODIE COULDN'T GET to Jennifer fast enough. His hands were pounding on the dashboard. "Hurry, Davis—hurry the hell up!"

The car screeched around the corner, and Davis slammed hard on his brakes in front of what looked like an old garage. Brodie rushed out of the car—

And heard a gunshot.

His heart stopped then. Just stopped in his chest even as his legs pistoned and he raced toward the building.

He heard Davis yelling after him. Telling him to

be careful, to go in slow, but he couldn't slow down. Jennifer was in there, and that gunshot blast still thundered through his mind.

Don't be dead. Don't be—

He kicked the door open. Brodie knew the sight before him would haunt his nightmares for the rest of his life.

Shayne was on the floor. Blood soaked the area around him, and his friend wasn't moving. A gun was a few inches from his open palm.

Stephen Brushard was there. The guy had changed one hell of a lot from the picture that Brodie had seen, but he still recognized him. His eyes were the same—even if his face was a haggard shell of the man he'd been. Brushard had his gun aimed at Jennifer. Jennifer...bleeding, hurt, her face so pale and her eyes so desperate as she looked at Brodie with hope and horror plain to see on her beautiful face. She was struggling against her binds, and he saw her kick free of the ropes around her legs.

"Stay away from her!" Brodie yelled.

Stephen laughed. "I don't have to get closer. She can die right here."

The hell she could. "Drop your weapon!"

"That's what the dirty cop said, too," Stephen taunted him. "Guess how that ended?"

The guy's weapon was pointed right at Jennifer.

"Are you trying to decide," Stephen asked, "if you can kill me *before* I kill her? I mean, even if you get the shot off at me first…won't my finger just spasm around the trigger and I'll still wind up killing her? Are you thinking about that? Are you realizing that you can't do any—"

"Roll!" Brodie roared.

Jennifer rolled her body.

Brodie fired. The bullet sank into Stephen's chest. The man fired then, his bullet exploding from the weapon as his finger jerked on the trigger.

But Jennifer was still rolling away from Shayne's still form. Stephen's bullets just blasted into the cement floor, missing her.

Davis rushed in behind Brodie—even as Stephen fell to his knees.

Carefully, Brodie closed in on his prey. A big circle of blood was blooming on Stephen's chest, but the guy was still alive. And he still had his weapon.

"Drop your gun," Brodie said again.

Stephen's head tilted back. His eyes were wide, blazing. "She…dies…" He tried to lift his gun again.

Brodie fired.

This time, Stephen's body hit the floor.

"No," Brodie said softly. "She doesn't."

Davis ran around him and kicked the guy's gun away.

Brodie knew Brushard wasn't a threat to anyone, not anymore. He turned his back on him and ran toward Jennifer. "Sweetheart?" He caught her shoulders and lifted her up. She was bleeding and shaking, and the terror he felt seemed to claw him apart.

"Just like…before…" Jennifer whispered. "Rushed in…to find me…"

Her hands were cuffed behind her. Where were the keys? "What did he do?"

"Knife…" Her lips trembled. Tears leaked from her eyes. "Didn't think I'd…see you again…"

"He's dead," Davis said flatly, and Brodie heard his footsteps shuffle closer.

Brodie pressed a hard, frantic kiss to Jennifer's quivering lips. "Like I would have let you go." *Never.* He shoved the gun into the back of his waistband. Then his hands slid over her. There was so much blood on Jennifer. Too much. He lifted her into his arms, holding her close against his chest, his heart. *She's alive. She's alive. She's alive.*

He put his forehead to hers and tried to breathe.

"Sorry…" A hoarse whisper.

With Jennifer in his arms, he turned and saw that Davis was now bent over Shayne. His friend's eyes were cracked open. Davis had his hands on Shayne's chest, and he was trying to halt the terrible blood flow.

"Didn't mean…for them to die…" Shayne managed. "Not…them…"

Brodie saw Davis's body tense. "Did Stephen Brushard kill our parents?"

"N-no…"

"Did you kill our parents?" Davis asked, voice hoarse as he kept applying pressure on the wound. Kept trying to save the man who'd been a friend to them both for so long.

Who they'd *thought* had been a friend.

"No…"

"Do you know who did?" Davis demanded. "Damn it, *tell us*!"

Sirens screeched outside. Doors slammed. Footsteps pounded toward them.

Shayne whispered something to Davis.

"What?" Davis demanded. *"What?"*

But Shayne wasn't saying anymore. Davis kept pushing on his chest, ordering the man to talk.

Cops burst into the garage. Brodie just held Jennifer tighter. To him, she was the thing that mattered most right then. Not finding his parents' killer.

"I can't lose you," he said.

He turned away as the EMTs rushed in to work on Shayne. He carried Jennifer out of that garage. Hands reached for her, but he was the one who put her in the ambulance. He couldn't let her go.

He laid her on the stretcher. Pushed her hair away from her cheek. A young EMT with blond hair and nervous hands quickly started inspecting Jennifer's wounds.

"You keep saving me…" Jennifer whispered as she looked up at Brodie. "That's a…habit you have."

He bent, pressed a kiss to her lips. That bastard

Brushard had shot her and used his knife on her. He could see the injuries now as the EMT tried to assess her. In that instant, Brodie wanted to kill the man all over again.

"Didn't I tell you before?" he whispered back to her. "You can always count me on."

She tried to smile for him, and that sight broke his heart.

The heart that was hers. Did she know it was?

The ambulance's siren echoed around them.

"I love you, Jenny," he said.

Her eyes widened. She shook her head.

"I. Love. You."

His fingers twined with hers. "And I'll say it over and over, for the rest of my life." A life that wouldn't have mattered much at all if he'd gotten into that garage too late. If he'd lost her...

No.

"Sir, are you coming with us to the hospital?" the EMT asked. "Or are you staying at the scene?"

He didn't look away from Jennifer. She needed him. *And I need her.* It didn't matter if the secrets he wanted were in that garage. The woman he loved was right in front of him. "I'm coming with you."

The ambulance started moving.

"I love you," he told Jennifer again, and his hold tightened on her.

DAVIS WATCHED AS Detective Shayne Townsend was loaded into the back of an ambulance. The EMTs were working frantically on him, but he wasn't responding to them.

Davis knew a killing wound when he saw one—hell, he'd seen plenty during the field as a SEAL. Shayne wasn't going to survive. The friend he'd known for years… Hell, Shayne was already gone.

And he took his secrets with him.

"Davis!"

He turned at the shout, and Davis saw his brother Grant running toward him. But the cops had just put up a band of yellow police tape, and they tried to keep Grant back.

Grant's gaze fell on the body that was being wheeled out. A body that was carefully covered. Pain flashed on Grant's face right before he shoved at the cops and snarled, "My brothers were in there! My—"

Davis hurried toward him. "That's not Brodie. He's fine."

Grant sucked in a sharp gulp of air. "Where is he?"

"He went to the hospital with Jennifer." His twin's face had been so terrified as he held Jennifer, clutching her tightly against his chest.

"Is she…is she going to make it?" Grant asked carefully. Grant would understand just how terrified

Brodie felt. Davis had watched Grant go through a similar hell when the woman Grant loved, Scarlett, had been attacked months before.

"I think so." She'd better survive. He wasn't sure what Brodie would do without her.

I don't want to find out.

Guilt already ate at him. It was his fault that Jennifer had been taken. He'd known how important she was to his twin, but when the threat had been at hand, he hadn't protected her.

Instead, Jennifer had saved *him*. He owed her now, more than he could ever repay.

"Shayne is the one who won't make it." Davis fought to keep the emotion from his voice. "I think the shot… It was too close to his heart." The ambulance was racing away, but Davis knew the doctors wouldn't be much good.

He glanced down at his hands and saw Shayne's blood covering his fingers.

SHE HURT. THE PAIN rolled through Jennifer in waves that just wouldn't stop. She could see Stephen, coming right at her with his knife. He'd put the blade to her face and—

Her scream woke her.

"Easy."

And *he* was there, catching her hand. Bringing it to his lips and kissing her fingers.

"You're safe, sweetheart," Brodie told her softly. "I've got you. No one can hurt you. Not ever again."

The machines around her beeped frantically, a loud chorus that made her head ache. "My face…"

Brodie frowned at her.

"He was cutting me…to match his wounds."

His jaw hardened.

"He was cutting my face… He was going to kill me."

He caught her chin and stared deeply into her eyes. "He's dead. You don't have to worry about him ever again."

She swallowed and tried to calm her racing heartbeat. Despite the frantic drumming of her heart, Jennifer's body felt sluggish. She felt the pull of an IV on her wrist. "You killed him?"

He nodded. It was wrong to be glad a man was dead. Wasn't it? But she didn't feel bad. She just felt relief. She wasn't being hunted by him. She was free.

The pain medicine they'd given her was pulling Jennifer under, but she managed to ask, "Shayne?"

"He's dead."

She swallowed. "Saved me…not all bad." She felt Brodie brush back her hair. "Sorry…you lost him…"

Her eyes closed. He pressed a kiss to her cheek.

"I wouldn't have made it," he whispered, his words following her, "if I'd lost you."

Chapter Twelve

She was finally out of the hospital. No more miserable hospital food and people poking at her all during the day and night.

Jennifer stood on the bluff at the McGuire ranch. The lake was still and beautiful. Perfect. She pulled in a deep gulp of fresh air as she tried to calm her nerves.

The doctors had told her that she was free to go, and Jennifer knew that it was, indeed, time for her to go…time to leave Austin. Time to leave Brodie.

Stephen found me. He tracked me down. Hurt so many people.

But Stephen wasn't the only man she'd helped to put away. What if others came after her? What if they did something to hurt Brodie? His family?

No, she couldn't take that risk.

It's time to say goodbye.

"Beautiful," Brodie murmured from beside her.

She nodded, still staring at the lake and trying to gather her courage for what she had to say. "It is."

"I'm not talking about the lake."

Her gaze flew toward him, and she found Brodie staring right at her. With his eyes on her, he closed the distance between them. His hand slipped beneath her chin, and he kissed her. Softly. Sensually.

Jennifer leaned into him. He'd been at the hospital with her, nearly every single moment. But he'd been so careful with her there. Every touch had seemed restrained even as every glance he'd sent her way had been filled with a desperate need.

She could feel the power in his body. Taste the desire in his kiss.

"Davis isn't here," Brodie told her. "It's just you and me." He stepped back. "Come inside with me?"

She should tell him goodbye now. Walk away even as she shattered on the inside, but Jennifer nodded. *I can't leave him, not yet.* Their hands entwined as they went back to the ranch house.

Then they were inside his bedroom. Her clothes fell to the floor. His hand slid over her, learning every inch of her body once more.

He was still dressed. Still wearing his shirt and his jeans, and that just wasn't going to do for her.

She pushed up his shirt. Her fingers slid along the hard, muscled expanse of his abs. Seconds later, Brodie's shirt went sailing through the air, and she kissed his chest, loving the power that he held so easily. Her fingers pulled on his belt. Unhooked the snap of his jeans. His aroused length pressed against her. Hot and hard. Her fingers curled around him, and she stroked him, pumping his flesh. She loved the way he responded to her. Loved the hard growl that broke from him and the way his body tensed beneath her touch.

When he tried to take control, she pushed him back onto the bed, and Jennifer slowly crawled on top of him. Her knees pressed into the mattress as her hips pressed down on him. They were flesh to flesh, just the way she wanted him, but she wasn't taking him into her body. Not yet.

She wanted to enjoy him more.

Jennifer wanted this moment to last as long as possible because this would be their final time together. *I don't want to leave Brodie.* She wanted to spend the rest of her life with him.

Jennifer bent toward him, and her hair swept down, falling around them. She pressed a kiss to his neck. Her tongue licked his skin. His hands were around her, sliding down her back, urging her closer. So close.

She kissed her way down his chest. Licked his nipples and heard the reward of his ragged groan.

Down, down she went as she learned every inch of his body, just as he'd learned hers before. There were no secrets between them. Only pleasure.

Her mouth pressed to his aroused flesh. She—

Was on her back. He'd rolled her in a lightning-fast move, and he had her carefully pinned beneath him.

"Sweetheart, you're driving me out of my mind."

Then his hand was between her legs. She arched toward him because his touch felt so good. He was stroking her, moving those wicked fingers against the center of her need, and her release rushed up, strong and hot just as he pulled his hand back and drove into her.

Time seemed to stop right in that moment. She was on the precipice of pleasure but trapped by his gaze. Then he kissed her, and the world exploded as his hips pushed hard against her. Again and again, he thrust into her, and the climax surged through her. So strong, so powerful, that Jennifer lost her breath. Her nails dug into his back, and she locked her legs around him.

He kept thrusting. Kept driving toward release.

And when she was sure her body couldn't take any more, when she was limp and trembling and sweat coated his body...

Then the desire grew again. He withdrew and drove deep.

And she held tightly to him.

I don't want to leave. I want to stay with Brodie... forever.

EVEN THOUGH THE lamp spilled light into the room, Jennifer knew it was dark outside. The sun had set long ago. She'd lost herself to hours of pleasure with Brodie.

She could slip away in the darkness. She *should* slip away.

But Jennifer couldn't take her gaze off him. They were tangled together in bed. His arm was over her stomach, her leg over his. The sheet had fallen to his waist.

As she stared at him, she thought, as she had so long before...

Sleep makes him look innocent. Sleep took away the hard intensity of his eyes. Sleep softened the warrior.

Almost helplessly, her hand rose and her fingers smoothed over the dark stubble that lined his jaw. At her touch, his eyes opened, and that green stare wasn't the least bit foggy. He was 100 percent awake and aware.

And it's time for me to leave.

"Thank you," Jennifer whispered, and it was as if she were trapped back in the past. Saying good-bye to him all over again at that little safe house. "Thank you for saving me." *I thought I was going to die.* Just like before. Her chest ached.

He didn't say a word, just stared at her as the lamp's light fell onto the bed.

Being with him then...it was so much like before, when they'd been in the Middle East. She hadn't wanted to leave him then.

Will I ever see you again? Years ago, that question had been pulled from her.

But then, he'd told her…*Hopefully, you won't need to see me.*

Yet she'd hoped to see him.

Try not to get kidnapped again, and you won't need me.

Danger was a part of her life. A part that she wouldn't push into his world. Not anymore.

She attempted to smile because she didn't want him to see just how much this was hurting her.

"No." His hard growl had her smile freezing.

Then vanishing.

"You aren't leaving me," Brodie told her as he rose up from the bed.

She grabbed for the sheet and held it carefully to her breasts as she suddenly felt far too vulnerable next to him.

"I had to watch you walk away before. I had to wonder about you for *years*." His head came toward hers. "That's not happening again. I can't go through that hell again."

"Brodie—"

"Do you even remember what I said to you? When I was carrying you out of that damn blood-filled garage?"

No, she didn't. Things had been kind of foggy then, what with the blood loss and the panic and the shock.

"I. Love. You."

She shook her head. Was she still in shock? Because Jennifer thought she'd heard him say—

"I love you," he said again, the words softer but the expression in his eyes just as hard.

"You can't," Jennifer whispered back as she tightened her hold on that sheet. "You don't…you don't know me." No one did. Jennifer Wesley wasn't real. She—

"I love Jennifer Wesley. I love Jenny Belmont. I love the woman who goes wild in my arms. I love the woman who risks her life for my family. I love the woman that I hold in the night. The woman who makes me smile even when I want to explode. *I love you.*"

"I'm not safe." Her words seemed far too soft. She cleared her throat and tried again. "Stephen found me. What if others do, too? What if—"

"If anyone ever comes after you again, I will be right there, standing at your side."

He wasn't listening to her. *I love you.* And his words were all she could hear. "I don't want you put at risk."

"I can handle risk."

"Your family—"

He had her caged between the headboard and his body. "What do you think I'll do without you?"

She didn't want to think about her life without

him. So much had changed for her in just a few short days. No, *he'd* changed everything.

"You came to me because you thought you could trust me. You thought I'd help keep you safe."

Jennifer nodded.

"Sweetheart, I will spend the rest of my life loving you and keeping you safe. Making you happy. Doing anything you want." His gaze searched hers. "I can't watch you walk away again. I told you that before, in that damn police station."

He didn't understand. She was trying to do what was right. "I never should have brought my danger to your door. If Sullivan had been killed, if Davis had—"

"They weren't, and we can do what-ifs all day long, but they don't change anything. The fact is…I love you, and I'd take any risk to be with you."

But would he really risk his family? No, that just wasn't Brodie. For him, family always came first.

He swore, obviously reading her fears on her face. "If you leave, then I'm just going to come with you."

And leave his family? "No!"

"I can vanish with you, or you can stay here and build a life with me. Those are the choices."

He would really give up everything for her?

"Unless…" Now she saw a flash of vulnerability in his eyes. She'd never seen him look vulnerable before. Not Brodie. "Unless you don't love me. Unless you don't want to be with me—"

She put her hands on his cheeks and she kissed him. Deeply. Wildly. The same way she loved him. "I love you," Jennifer whispered against his lips. "More than anything."

His shoulders slumped. "Then stay with me. We can make it work. We can make anything work if we're together."

"If something else happened to your family because of me…" With the past already between them, with his parents' death… "Brodie, I couldn't handle that. You couldn't handle it."

He pulled back just a little and stared down at her with blazing eyes. "You didn't do it. You weren't responsible for what happened to my parents."

"But I brought Stephen—"

"My brother asked Shayne if he killed my parents. In his final moments, he said he didn't."

Jennifer's breath caught in her throat.

"Then Davis asked him…he asked him if he knew who had killed them…"

Pain came then, flashing over his face.

"Brodie?"

"The last thing Shayne said was…Montgomery."

She started to shake her head—

"The Montgomery ranch is right next door. Mark Montgomery's father…he killed himself two months after my parents died. The puzzle pieces are all there. We just have to figure them out." His hands tightened on her arms. "We *will* figure them out."

Her heart ached as she stared at him.

"We know Brushard had a man in the area back then—the same man who was watching you. We will track him down. We'll get all of his photos, learn everything he saw. Every day, we will get closer to finding out what really happened to my parents."

She wanted closure for him because every time he mentioned his parents, she could see the pain in his eyes.

"I can face anything," Brodie told her, "any damn thing, as long as I have you. Please, Jennifer, don't leave again. Stay with me. If danger comes, then we'll be ready for it. Hell, sweetheart, I'm a SEAL. I'm the best man you can have at your side when hell comes calling."

He was the only man she wanted at her side, and in her bed, for the rest of her life.

The only man in her heart.

"Stay?" he asked softly, his mouth just inches from her own.

She thought about the past six years. About the times she'd caught herself looking over her shoulder, looking for him.

Life wasn't about fear. It wasn't about regret.

So she stared into his eyes, she saw the love there, and Jennifer whispered, "Yes."

Because he was right. They would face any danger coming their way. Together. He would fight for her, she knew it, and Jennifer would do anything to protect him and his family.

Her SEAL had given her a second chance. She was going to take that chance, and they'd see where the future led them.

This time, her love was stronger than her fear.

This time…she held him tightly. She didn't let go.

And she knew that finally, *finally*, with Brodie… she was home.

Epilogue

Mark Montgomery had been Davis McGuire's friend for as long as Davis could remember.

Davis trusted him just as much as he trusted his brothers.

But then...he'd trusted Shayne Townsend, too.

Davis stood back. His brothers were at his side, his sister close by. They all watched as Shayne Townsend was laid to rest. He turned his head and glanced over at Brodie. His twin's face was hard, tense. Jennifer was at Brodie's side, her arms around him.

Jennifer Wesley. She'd come into their lives like a cyclone, and she'd changed Brodie's world. There would be no going back for Brodie, not now.

I want to marry her. Brodie had told him that the night before. *But Jennifer's scared... She worries her past might hurt me.*

Brodie wasn't going to let anyone or anything hurt his lady.

Davis's gaze slid to the right. To Mark Montgomery. Mark was staring at the grave site with an expression much like Brodie's. Hard. Tense. Angry.

But then Mark moved…shifted…and his stare locked on Davis's sister, Ava.

Davis saw the flash of longing there. Davis had seen that same longing in Mark's gaze before, but Mark had never made a move to touch Ava.

And I'm damned glad of that fact.

Because after Shayne's dying words, Davis didn't know if he was looking at a friend…

Or at a killer.

The service ended. The crowd started to slip away. But Mark…Mark closed in on Ava.

"Ava, we need to talk," Mark said softly.

Ava glanced up at him, and for just a moment, Davis could have sworn he saw a flash of longing in her eyes, too.

Hell. He stepped forward, aware that his brothers were all following his lead. They knew about Shayne's last words, but they hadn't told them to Ava. Not yet. They wanted to do more digging first.

But it looked as if they might have just run out of time…

Because Mark appeared to be done with waiting.

Davis stepped in front of Ava. "Stay away from her," he told his friend.

"What?" Mark looked at him as if Davis had lost his mind.

Maybe he had, but Davis wasn't about to lose his sister, too.

"We know, Mark," Davis said. "Shayne told us." It was a deliberate push, to see what Mark would reveal.

But Mark just shook his head. "You don't know anything." He leaned in close to Davis. "And you *aren't* going to keep me away from Ava. I'm done waiting."

The words were a threat, and Davis tensed, more than ready to do battle.

"Not here," Brodie said, grabbing his arm. "Not now."

He'd almost forgotten they were at a cemetery and the grieving were all around them.

Mark stepped back. He gave a curt nod, then turned on his heel and stalked away.

Ava yanked Davis around to face her. "What are you doing? Are you crazy?" she demanded. Ava was small, delicate, an exact opposite of her brothers. But she had the McGuire eyes—green and glinting with emotion.

"Ava…" Hell, he didn't know what to say then. "Mark isn't… He may not be the man you think."

Her gaze hardened. "And maybe he is." She stepped back from him. "Maybe he's exactly what I need." Her voice was determined.

Then Ava straightened her shoulders. She turned

away. Walked slowly and carefully and left him behind without a backward glance.

"We're going to have trouble," Grant muttered.

Yes, they were.

But no one was going to hurt Ava. Davis would
keep her safe, no matter what.

*Even if I have to battle another friend...I will.
I will protect my sister, at all costs...*

* * * * *

LARGER-PRINT BOOKS!

GET 2 FREE LARGER-PRINT NOVELS PLUS

2 FREE GIFTS!

✦ HARLEQUIN®

Romance

From the Heart, For the Heart

YES! Please send me 2 FREE LARGER-PRINT Harlequin® Romance novels and my 2 FREE gifts (gifts are worth about $10). After receiving them, if I don't wish to receive any more books, I can return the shipping statement marked "cancel." If I don't cancel, I will receive 4 brand-new novels every month and be billed just $4.84 per book in the U.S. or $5.24 per book in Canada. That's a savings of at least 19% off the cover price! It's quite a bargain! Shipping and handling is just 50¢ per book in the U.S. and 75¢ per book in Canada.* I understand that accepting the 2 free books and gifts places me under no obligation to buy anything. I can always return a shipment and cancel at any time. Even if I never buy another book, the two free books and gifts are mine to keep forever.

119/319 HDN F43Y

Name _____ (PLEASE PRINT) _____

Address _____ Apt. # _____

City _____ State/Prov. _____ Zip/Postal Code _____

Signature (if under 18, a parent or guardian must sign)

Mail to the **Harlequin® Reader Service:**
IN U.S.A.: P.O. Box 1867, Buffalo, NY 14240-1867
IN CANADA: P.O. Box 609, Fort Erie, Ontario L2A 5X3

Want to try two free books from another line?
Call 1-800-873-8635 or visit www.ReaderService.com.

* Terms and prices subject to change without notice. Prices do not include applicable taxes. Sales tax applicable in N.Y. Canadian residents will be charged applicable taxes. Offer not valid in Quebec. This offer is limited to one order per household. Not valid for current subscribers to Harlequin Romance Larger-Print books. All orders subject to credit approval. Credit or debit balances in a customer's account(s) may be offset by any other outstanding balance owed by or to the customer. Please allow 4 to 6 weeks for delivery. Offer available while quantities last.

Your Privacy—The Harlequin® Reader Service is committed to protecting your privacy. Our Privacy Policy is available online at www.ReaderService.com or upon request from the Harlequin Reader Service.

We make a portion of our mailing list available to reputable third parties that offer products we believe may interest you. If you prefer that we not exchange your name with third parties, or if you wish to clarify or modify your communication preferences, please visit us at www.ReaderService.com/consumerschoice or write to us at Harlequin Reader Service Preference Service, P.O. Box 9062, Buffalo, NY 14269. Include your complete name and address.

HRLP13R

LARGER-PRINT BOOKS!
GET 2 FREE LARGER-PRINT NOVELS PLUS
2 FREE GIFTS!

HARLEQUIN

super romance

More Story...More Romance

LARGER-PRINT BOOKS!

HARLEQUIN *Presents*

PASSION GUARANTEED SEDUCTION

GET 2 FREE LARGER-PRINT NOVELS PLUS 2 FREE GIFTS!

YES! Please send me 2 FREE LARGER-PRINT Harlequin Presents® novels and my 2 FREE gifts (gifts are worth about $10). After receiving them, if I don't wish to receive any more books, I can return the shipping statement marked "cancel." If I don't cancel, I will receive 6 brand-new novels every month and be billed just $5.05 per book in the U.S. or $5.49 per book in Canada. That's a saving of at least 16% off the cover price! It's quite a bargain! Shipping and handling is just 50¢ per book in the U.S. and 75¢ per book in Canada.* I understand that accepting the 2 free books and gifts places me under no obligation to buy anything. I can always return a shipment and cancel at any time. Even if I never buy another book, the two free books and gifts are mine to keep forever.

176/376 HDN F43N

Name _____ (PLEASE PRINT)

Address _____ Apt. #

City _____ State/Prov. _____ Zip/Postal Code

Signature (if under 18, a parent or guardian must sign)

Mail to the **Harlequin® Reader Service:**
IN U.S.A.: P.O. Box 1867, Buffalo, NY 14240-1867
IN CANADA: P.O. Box 609, Fort Erie, Ontario L2A 5X3

Are you a subscriber to Harlequin Presents books and want to receive the larger-print edition? Call 1-800-873-8635 today or visit us at www.ReaderService.com.

HPLP13R

ReaderService.com

Manage your account online!

- Review your order history
- Manage your payments
- Update your address

*We've designed
the Harlequin® Reader Service
website just for you.*

Enjoy all the features!

- Reader excerpts from any series
- Respond to mailings and
  special monthly offers
- Discover new series available to you
- Browse the Bonus Bucks catalog
- Share your feedback

Visit us at:
ReaderService.com

RS13